I0891402

MASSACRE CREEK

Center Point
Large Print

Also by Wayne C. Lee and available from Center Point Large Print:

Devil Wire
Showdown at Julesburg Station
Hawks of Autumn
Arikaree War Cry
Barbed-Wire War
The Fast Gun

MASSACRE CREEK

Wayne C. Lee

CENTER POINT LARGE PRINT
THORNDIKE, MAINE

This Center Point Large Print edition
is published in the year 2025 by arrangement with
Golden West Inc.

Copyright © 1985 by Wayne C. Lee.

All rights reserved.

This book is a work of fiction. All names, characters, places, and events are either products of the author's imagination or are used fictitiously. Any resemblance to actual events or locales or persons, living or dead, is entirely coincidental.

The text of this Large Print edition is unabridged.
In other aspects, this book may vary
from the original edition.
Printed in the United States of America
on permanent paper sourced using
environmentally responsible foresting methods.
Set in 16-point Times New Roman type.

ISBN: 979-8-89164-728-2

The Library of Congress has cataloged this record
under Library of Congress Control Number: 2025941706

MASSACRE CREEK

I

Lane Perry was stalking an antelope when he heard the first shot coming from the direction of the little wagon train. He leaped to his feet and the antelope, which had been moving cautiously toward the white rag Lane had been waving above the grass, wheeled and scampered toward the knoll where his little herd had been watching. Now the other animals joined their leader in loping over the hill, out of sight.

Lane forgot the antelope that he had been hoping to shoot for meat for the wagon train. He knew that Indians had killed white men here, along the Platte River, the last few years. But recently there had not been any real trouble.

All the same, Lane's first thought was that Indians had struck again and his concern was for his younger brother back at the train. Chris was only twenty, but he and Lane had been through a lot together. They had been separated during the war, but as soon as they both got home, they had headed west to the mountains to make their fortunes in the gold and silver fields. It hadn't worked out.

Lane ran to his horse now, jammed the rifle into its boot, and swung into the saddle. He estimated he was a mile from the train. He hoped the men were making a good defense, but there were only four wagons with just one man to a wagon. Lane and Chris were the only ones without a wagon. They had joined the train when it left Denver because they didn't want to travel alone on their way back to their Missouri home. Jud Bumbry, the leader of the train, needed a hunter to supply meat and there wasn't a spare man to hunt since each one had a wagon to drive. Lane and Chris took the hunting job, with Lane doing most of the work. He was the better shot and three years older than Chris.

Lane's horse moved quickly as the shooting up ahead grew louder. It sounded like a battle now. There were only five men with the wagons, and there were certainly a lot more rifles than that booming down there.

As Lane neared the valley the wagons had been following at noon today, he realized the shooting was coming from farther up. He had objected to leaving the regular trail early this morning and following a side valley to the south. But Jud Bumbry had said his wagon contained some freight for a man at the head of this valley, and he was going to deliver it. He insisted that all the wagons stay together for protection, and he also intended to make a circle to hit the main road farther down the river after he had delivered his freight.

The other three drivers objected to the extra

miles, but Jud Bumbry was the elected boss and he ran the little train with an iron hand. Lane and Chris carried little weight in any decisions. Their objections could hardly count since they were riding horses, not driving wagons.

Likely the Indians had seen the four wagons leave the main trail and had struck like wolves picking on a buffalo calf that had strayed from its herd. Lane blamed Jud Bumbry for this battle.

Reining up the valley, following the tracks the wagons had made in the grass, Lane was wishing he'd sent Chris on the hunt today. Lane would be more help with the wagons than Chris would.

A scene flashed across his mind that had taken place just a couple of days before they left Denver. Chris put faith in fortune-tellers; Lane didn't. They had been walking down Larimer Street when Chris had spotted a sign in a window advertising a fortune-teller in the building. Against his better judgment, Lane went in with Chris.

In a little cubbyhole in one corner of the building, the fortune-teller held sway. Chris had his fortune told, and the woman said things were so hazy she really couldn't tell him anything about his future. At Chris's insistence, Lane let her tell his fortune. She saw his future clearly, she said. He would get rich, but he would be in real danger before he achieved his wealth.

Lane shrugged off the prediction, but Chris worried about his "hazy" future. A chill ran over

Lane. If he had any faith in fortune-tellers, he would be very scared right now. That sounded like a vicious battle up ahead, and Chris was surely involved. He'd only been in a couple of battles in the war. He'd been too young to get into most of it. Lane had been in more battles than he cared to remember. He wished he could change places with Chris right now. Chris might be in more trouble than he could handle.

Suddenly the firing up ahead stopped. Lane listened carefully, but all he heard now was the thud of his horse's hoofs. He eased back his pace. He couldn't be quite sure how far he was from the wagons with no sounds to guide him. He wanted to see before he was seen.

The wagons had traveled a long way from the main road along the river. The shots might not even be heard on the road if there happened to be any traffic at the end of this long valley right at this moment.

A tiny creek bubbled along the middle of the valley and some willows and small bunches of cottonwoods grew along its banks. Lane could believe that someone might live along this creek somewhere, but he didn't understand Jud Bumbry's insistence that he deliver the freight directly to the man. He could have left it at Fort McPherson, which couldn't be too many miles down the river, and the man could have come there and gotten it. Bringing freight east from

Denver helped pay the way for the men going home. It was about all they had gotten out of their venture to the gold fields.

The valley made a slight turn, heading almost straight south just ahead, and Lane brought his horse down to a walk. Guessing from the shots he had heard, he might come in sight of the wagons when he turned that bend.

He saw the first of the wagons a moment later. He reined up his horse quickly and backed him out of sight. Then he dismounted and tied his horse to a twenty-foot cottonwood where he couldn't be seen.

Cautiously Lane moved ahead then, staying in the willows that hugged the creek between the cottonwoods. They weren't too big, but they offered protection for him.

There were men running around among the wagons, but the battle was over. Lane studied the men. He was still some distance from them, but he was close enough to know those weren't the men he'd been traveling with the last two weeks. They were white men, too, not Indians.

There could be only one reason for this raid, Lane thought. Robbery. But what could the wagons be carrying that would be worth robbing? He hadn't been aware of anything unusual in the wagons. Of course, he hadn't examined their contents.

Lane had to get closer. Where were the men

with the wagons? And where was Chris? Had they abandoned the wagons in order to make a stand somewhere? Lane tried to believe that, but he couldn't. Those men running around among the wagons were not worried about a counter-attack.

Moving carefully through the willows, Lane got within a hundred yards of the nearest wagon. The wagons were strung out just as they had been traveling. Now he was close enough to see the men who had been with the wagons. He counted four, all apparently dead. There had been five. Where was the fifth one?

His first hope was that Chris was the missing one. Maybe he had escaped on his horse. But that bubble burst when Lane saw Chris's horse standing close to the second wagon. Then the last glimmer of hope vanished when he recognized one of the men rummaging through the wagons. It was Jud Bumbry, the boss of the little wagon train.

Lane stared at Bumbry. He was poking through the wagons just like the others. The truth struck Lane then. Bumbry was one of the bandits. He had betrayed every man in the train. There was no man in this valley waiting for a delivery from Bumbry's wagon other than these bandits.

If Bumbry was alive, then one of the four who appeared to be dead had to be Chris, unless the men with the wagons had managed to kill one of the outlaws. That didn't seem very likely, with Bumbry calling the shots and being in league with the outlaws. The attack had likely been a complete surprise to all but Bumbry.

But why had the gang killed all the drivers? What could possibly be in those wagons that would be worth a massacre?

Fighting back a strong urge to rush out there and see if Chris might still be alive, Lane tried to make a reasonable assessment of the situation. This was a band of outlaws who wanted something from these wagons bad enough to murder everybody in the train to get it. Lane was a member of that train, but he had been away when the strike was made. If they found him, he'd be killed, too. Of that he was sure.

But that didn't seem to matter much to him right now. Chris was what mattered. Lane had always been a protector of sorts of his younger brother. And today, when Chris needed him most, he hadn't been here. Through his grief, one thing hammered at Lane. Somebody would pay for the murder of his brother.

Lane remembered that Jud Bumbry hadn't really wanted Chris and Lane to join the wagon train in Denver. They had almost begged for a chance to go with the train because they wanted to get back home and traveling alone on horseback did not seem the safest way to go.

Only when Bumbry was reminded that someone

needed to hunt for food for the men did he relent and take them in. Lane guessed that Bumbry knew right then that every man going with him was going to die before the end of the trip. The fewer men he had with him, the less danger there would be that someone in the attacking party would be killed. It appeared that none of the attackers had died in this ambush.

Lane fingered his gun. If he could get a little closer, he might try to kill Bumbry. But reason slowly took over. He could count five men there. He'd have no chance against that many.

He watched the men as they ripped things out of the wagons. They didn't seem to be interested in the items they were dumping on the ground. Maybe there was something hidden under the freight that they wanted.

He inched a little closer so he could see the men better. Other than Jud Bumbry, there were four men in sight.

One man of the four stood out. He wasn't quite as big as Bumbry, but that was not unusual. Jud Bumbry was almost six and a half feet tall and weighed in the neighborhood of two hundred and eighty pounds, a big, dark-skinned, black-eyed man that Lane had never fully trusted. Now Lane realized that he had trusted him too much.

The other prominent man there was a little over six feet tall, deeply tanned, and had a habit of jerking his head quickly from one thing to another as if he expected to catch someone doing something he wouldn't like. Lane wouldn't trust him with a pinch of salt.

The other three men poking through the wagons made little impression on Lane. He hated them all. They had been responsible for what had happened to Chris. He wanted to kill every one of them. But he knew that one or two, at the most, would be all he could get before he was killed. He couldn't make that kind of a trade. He'd wait. Somehow he'd get his chance even if he had to trail the killers for the next ten years.

Lane couldn't resist moving closer. He had to find out what the men were looking for. It didn't seem to be in the freight that the wagons were hauling. Since the wagons were coming from Denver, perhaps there was a shipment of gold from one of the mines there. Or possibly it was silver. Either would attract highwaymen. But if there was gold or silver in the wagons, nobody had mentioned it as they traveled east.

The men completely unloaded one wagon while Lane watched. They barely looked at the goods on the ground. One man got into the empty wagon and began tearing at the floorboards of the box.

Lane wondered if they thought there was gold under the floorboards. He had heard of one man who shipped his gold out under a false bottom in his wagon. But when the floorboards came up in this wagon, the man was looking right down at the ground. There was no false bottom in this wagon.

Lane couldn't keep his gun out of his hand. But he realized he was at the far edge of the revolver's range and the men kept milling around until he couldn't get Bumbry in his sights.

The men left that wagon and went to the next one, moving farther out of Lane's range. They started tearing everything out of that wagon.

Suddenly Bumbry stopped and straightened up. Lane could hear his words very clearly from where he was crouching in the willows.

"There was another man with the wagons," Bumbry shouted.

The other tall man wheeled on him. "What do you mean? We got rid of all the men here."

"There is one more," Bumbry said, a bit more quietly. "He went out to hunt for meat for the men about noon. I forgot about him."

"Forgot?" screamed the other man. "That's like forgetting your head."

"There's nothing one man can do, Easy," Bumbry said.

Lane tensed. That outlaw must be Easy Widlow. He'd heard of him. As bad a man as ever roamed the plains, he'd been told.

"You blithering idiot!" the outlaw yelled. "One man can call in the whole army. We're not too far from the fort, you know."

"We'll watch for him to come in," Bumbry said. "We'll get him then."

"Maybe he heard the shooting," another man said. "He could be close by right now."

"You can almost bet on that," Widlow said.

"Then we'd better get him before he gets away," Bumbry said.

The tall outlaw swore. "It was your idea to kill them all so there would be nobody to tell what happened. Too bad you didn't have sense enough to remember how many there were."

Bumbry scowled at the outlaw leader, but he didn't argue. "Let's see if he's around anywhere."

Widlow wheeled on the men. "Fan out. Look everywhere, especially down the creek. That's the way he's liable to come in."

"Let's just get out of here and let him go," one man suggested.

"You numbskull!" Widlow shouted. "We haven't found what we're looking for yet. Besides, if that man gets away after seeing what we did here, we could be in real trouble. A massacre like this is bound to bring out the army."

The men started away from the wagons. Two of them were coming toward Lane. He knew that if they found him, there would be no question what would happen to him. He'd be shot.

II

Lane, his gun in his hand, watched the men as they spread out from the wagons. He'd take one or two with him if they found him, but he knew that wasn't going to change the final outcome. There were five of them and there was no way he could win over that many.

One of the two men directly in front of Lane stopped and called over to the tall outlaw leader.

"He may already be gone. He could be on his way to the fort."

"If we don't find him," Widlow shouted back, "we'll have to expect that."

"He'll either be close by or still out on the hunt," Bumbry called. "He would never ride off without finding out for sure what happened to his brother. He's played nursemaid to him ever since we left Denver."

"Is he dangerous?" the second of the men directly in front of Lane asked.

"He's a hunter," Widlow said. "Figure it out for yourself."

Lane saw the hesitation in the men. He wished he had his rifle. He was better with that than he was with a revolver. But it was back in the boot on his saddle. It wasn't an easy thing to carry through cover if he wanted to move quietly.

There was no question in Lane's mind what he had to do. Some way he had to retreat to his horse without giving away his presence. Now that they were looking for him, that was going to be quite difficult.

If one of those men coming down along the willows had been Jud Bumbry, Lane would have waited for him and killed him, then taken a chance on escaping the others. But he had never seen either of the men who were walking very cautiously down either side of the strip of willows that bordered the creek.

He couldn't be sure which one of those five men had actually killed his brother, but he'd feel partially vindicated, at least, if he could kill Jud Bumbry. It had been Bumbry who had betrayed the wagon train. He was as much a part of Widlow's gang as any of the other three men who took Widlow's orders. Jud's double-crossing of the men under him made him the chief villain as far as Lane was concerned.

Lane more or less ignored the men who were moving out to the sides of the valley. Widlow and one of his men were taking the side to the west, the direction where Lane had been hunting this afternoon. Bumbry was moving east from the wagons. That was farther from Lane than any of the others. He'd have no chance at him.

The two outlaws assigned to search the willows along the creek seemed overly cautious. Perhaps

Widlow's warning that Lane was a hunter was having some effect on them. They were moving slowly, checking every couple of minutes with each other across the willows. In some places the willows were short enough so that the men could see each other over the tops of the little trees. In other places, the willows were too tall to see over.

Lane began retreating through the willows toward the place where he had tied his horse to the cottonwood around the bend in the valley. Every move had to be calculated carefully so he would not give away his position. He had to make sure he didn't bend the willows and tell the men something was moving there.

His progress was very slow, but the two men coming down either side of the willows were also moving at a snail's pace. When they came to a clump they couldn't see through, one of them moved up and cautiously peeked through the limbs while the other man stood with his gun ready.

Lane could see that he wasn't going to be able to hide and let the men pass him. He had to stay ahead of them. Once he checked to see where the other men were, but he couldn't see anyone on either side.

Lane began planning ahead. The two pursuers were being so cautious, he thought he could keep ahead of them. Once he got to his horse, he'd ride as hard as he could down the valley until he came to the land bordering the Platte River. Then he'd turn east until he hit Fort McPherson. He knew it couldn't be too far.

As Lane picked his way through the willows, he suddenly found himself exposed. There was a five-yard gap in the trees.

Lifting his head enough to see the men searching the willows behind him, he saw that they were forty yards upstream. His eyes shot to either side, but he saw none of the three men who had fanned out from the wagons. He had to take the chance.

Ducking as low as he could, Lane ran across the open space and slipped into a thicket of willows that hugged the bank of the creek. No shots came his way and he heard nothing to indicate that he'd been seen. He hoped he didn't encounter any more of those open spaces before he reached his horse.

He considered hiding here till the two men came to the open space. If he moved quickly and shot accurately, he could get both of them. But he'd give away his position. Those other men were close even if he couldn't see them. They'd come on the run if there were gunshots.

As the men came closer, Lane knew he had to move farther through the willows.

Then there was a yell from nearby. The men behind Lane jerked up their heads and looked, standing like statues. Lane turned his head and peered through parted branches of the willows. He couldn't see anything. But he did notice that he was near the curve in the valley. The yell must have come from around the corner.

Suddenly, he knew what the yell meant, and his heart sank. Someone had found his horse. To verify his conclusion, a man came around the bend, leading Lane's horse. Then Widlow came from the far side of the creek to join the man who had found the horse. Lane wondered if Bumbry would come, too.

His eyes switched back to the two men who had been stalking him. They had forgotten the search of the willows and were running toward the man with Lane's horse. They passed within a few feet of Lane as they ran down the valley. He remained low in the willows.

Lane was close enough to the meeting place of the four men that he could hear what they said. They'd almost certainly search the area close to the horse. He wouldn't have a chance of escaping them now. Even if he did, he'd be afoot.

"He's got to be around here somewhere," Widlow said.

"Maybe that isn't his horse," one man said.

"Whose else would it be?" Widlow shot back. "Nick and Dorse came down the creek, and you and me searched the side of the canyon over there."

"Maybe he was on Bumbry's side. If he was over there, Jud would surely find him. He really wants to make sure there are no survivors."

"Here comes Jud now," one of the men said. "Let's ask him."

"Sure," Widlow said and led the way up the valley to meet Jud Bumbry.

The caravan passed Lane and splashed across the creek in the open area just a few feet from him. But they were all concentrating on Jud Bumbry and not one even dropped a glance at the clump of willows immediately downstream.

The four met Bumbry several yards upstream from Lane's hiding place. "Ever see this horse before?" Widlow asked.

"Sure," Bumbry said. "That's Lane Perry's horse. He was riding him this afternoon when he went hunting."

"Then he's got to be around here somewhere," Widlow said.

"Evidently not close to his horse," one man said, "or he'd have lit a shuck out of here."

"Maybe he circled the wagons," another said. "Nobody looked up there."

"If he ain't there, he'll be hiding somewhere near," Bumbry agreed. "If we can't find him there, we'll come back and search this lower valley. He ain't going far without a horse."

The men turned up toward the wagons. Lane waited till they were some distance away. Then he inched his way downstream again. He tried not to make any movement visible to the men. One of them might look his way. Bumbry was right. There wasn't much he could do out here without a horse. But maybe he could survive long enough to think of some way out.

The men were moving quickly toward the wagons. When they didn't find him up there, they'd be back. They'd hunt him down like a crippled coyote. Bumbry seemed more determined than Easy Widlow that there be no witnesses to what had happened here.

Lane got around the corner of the valley and stopped, trying to relax. But he knew he had no time for that. He glanced up at the sun. It was nearing the western rim of the valley. It would be dark before long. If he could avoid detection until then, maybe he could get out of the valley on foot.

He didn't like that decision. Maybe he could get his horse back from the outlaws. That idea satisfied him better. But for now, he had to get out of sight. He was sure it wouldn't be long till all those men would be back down here searching for him.

Finding a side gully that ran out of the valley, he turned up it. There were no willows here, not even much brush or anything to hide in. He walked up the gully a short way and was surprised to find a hump that water had somehow run around in its rush to the creek after a rain. A low spot was behind that hump. It wasn't even visible from below. Lane tested the spot. If he lay flat, they couldn't see him from below. If they didn't come up this gully, they'd never find him. And from down there, the gully promised no surprises. It wasn't a perfect hiding place, but it was better than he had expected to find.

Going back to the main valley, Lane went to the corner where he could see the upper end. The men were spread out up there beyond the wagons, but, even as he watched, they began coming back toward the wagons.

Lane could almost read their minds. They were becoming convinced that he wasn't up there. That meant he had to be down here somewhere. His horse had been found here and he surely wouldn't have left without his horse.

Lane watched them start down the valley, keeping out of sight as he checked on their progress. He felt like a rabbit surrounded by coyotes. His only chance of survival was to hide.

He headed back for the gully and moved up behind the hump. There he stationed himself, listening carefully for any sound that would tell him the men were getting near.

They were on horses when they came this time. Lane hadn't expected that. It gave them a much better view of everything. He wondered if they would be able to see him lying flat behind this hump. He had convinced himself that a man on foot couldn't see him. But a man on horseback was something else.

Peeking cautiously over the top of the hump, Lane watched until the horses came into view. Then he flattened out behind the hump and hoped. He heard the horses stop, and voices, low and guarded, came to him. He couldn't make out what was being said, but he heard the squeak of leather as the riders moved closer. One or two were coming up the gully. The squeaking stopped.

"Ain't no sense in going any farther," one man growled. "We can see clear to the top of the gully. Ain't nobody in here."

"Yeah. We're sure of that. We'll take our time catching up. We'll tell Easy we went all the way to the top. What he don't know won't hurt him."

Lane hugged the ground and waited. After a couple of minutes, saddle leather squeaked again and the sound faded away. Lane lifted his head in time to see the two riders leave the gully and head down the valley.

Lane waited till darkness had shrouded the gully. Then he left his hiding place and moved down to the valley. He had heard horses going back up the valley just after dusk. Likely the outlaws would head into the canyons to the south of this area.

Turning up the valley, Lane headed for the wagons. This would be his chance to see for sure if all the men with the train were dead. But he hadn't gone more than halfway when he heard sounds ahead and knew that the men had not left the wagon area.

That changed Lane's plans. He would have no chance to check on the wagon drivers. Chances were a hundred to one that they were all dead now, anyway. If any had shown any signs of life, the outlaws would have snuffed it out quickly.

Lane had to get help. He didn't know how far away Fort McPherson was, but he knew it would take a long time to get there on foot, if he made it at all. He had to have a horse. His horse and the outlaws' horses, plus all the horses that had been pulling the wagons, were up there close to the wagons. But so were the outlaws. Nevertheless, Lane had to get a horse and there was only one way to do it.

Cautiously he circled the wrecked wagons, keeping well back in the shadows. He saw the men clustered around a small fire. Two of them were busy cooking some supper. It reminded Lane that he hadn't had anything to eat tonight, but he knew he wouldn't get any food. He concentrated on getting close to the horses without being detected.

Reason told him one of the men might be guarding the horses. Carefully Lane counted the shadows around the fire: four men. There should be five. That fifth one might be out here by the horses. Since they hadn't caught him, they might expect him to try to get a horse.

Lane got as close to the horses as he thought he dared until he made certain there was no guard or, if there was one, just where he was. It took ten minutes of studying the animals before he saw them raise their heads now and then to look a certain way. He followed the direction with his eyes and saw a dim figure leaning against a rock ledge along the edge of the valley. He seldom moved, but when he did, at least one of the horses usually lifted his head to look at him.

Knowing that those same movements of the horses might alert the guard to his presence, Lane glided as quietly and with as little motion as possible along the little rock bluff that protruded from the valley slope. Just as he reached an indentation in the little bluff, one of the horses apparently caught his movement and lifted his head and stared through the gloom at him. Lane shrank back into the depression in the bluff.

Glancing at the guard, he could see by the weak starlight that the man had noticed the horses and his eyes were searching the area where Lane was. Barely breathing, Lane waited to see what the guard would do.

The guard hesitated, looking from the horse to the bluff. Then he lifted his gun out of its holster and moved cautiously toward Lane. Lane had his own gun in his hand, but he didn't want to fire it. He would if he had to, to save his life, but he wouldn't get a horse if he did.

The guard came closer, his eyes searching the ground and the area ahead of him. Lane still waited. But the guard didn't see him hugging the bluff inside the depression. The guard stopped a few feet short of Lane's hiding place and, after sweeping the area with his eyes, turned back the way he had come.

It was Lane's chance and he took advantage of it. With three swift steps, he reached the guard and brought his gun barrel down over his head. The guard only grunted as he slid to the ground. The horses all lifted their heads and one snorted but then was quiet.

Lane waited to see if those at the campfire, which wasn't far away, noticed. But when they didn't change their attitudes, he edged toward the closest horse. In the dark, it was difficult to tell the saddle horses from the workhorses, but this one looked like a saddle horse. Then as he got closer, he discovered that there were five horses in a row here. All were saddled and fastened to a long rope. Lane didn't need to be told that they were expecting his visit.

As stealthily as possible, he approached the nearest horse, whispering softly to the animal. The horse watched him closely but didn't sidle away. Once he got a hand on his neck and petted him, the horse relaxed.

Lane didn't recognize him, so it wasn't either his or Chris's, but he didn't dare take time to try to pick out his own horse. He probably wasn't on the line, anyway.

Stepping up against the horse's side, he tightened the cinch on the saddle, then slipped the knot on the reins off the rope.

Slowly he started to lead the horse away, but the movement was detected at the fire.

"What are you doing, Nick?" one man called suspiciously.

"Moving this horse to better grass," Lane called back in a hoarse whisper.

He kept going, but he watched the men at the fire. They seemed to be whispering among themselves. Then one of them jumped up and started toward the line of horses on the run.

Lane sprang into the saddle and dug in his heels. The horse responded with a leap. A gun bellowed behind him and a shout rang out to get to the horses. Lane knew it would be a miracle if he got away.

III

Lane wished he'd had time to release the other saddled horses on the line, but he was lucky to get away at all. More shots came from the campfire and they snapped by dangerously close to him. He kicked his horse into its fastest run and was gratified to find that he had picked a good mount.

Lane headed down the valley. He had to get to Fort McPherson. The shots behind him stopped and in a minute were replaced by the thunder of hoofbeats. Having those horses saddled got the pursuit underway much faster.

Lane raced down the valley and around the curve, but he was shocked at the speed with which those behind him were coming. He wasn't gaining; in fact, he felt that he might be losing. It was dark enough that he couldn't see how close the pursuit was. He thought of the gully where he had hidden this afternoon. He couldn't hide a horse in there, but he might throw the pursuers off the track.

Reaching the gully, he reined his horse up into it, then stopped him so there would be no noise. If they had detected his move, he'd be in a trap. He got his gun in his hand and waited.

Within half a minute the horses thundered past the gully without hesitating. They hadn't noticed that he wasn't still ahead of them. The pounding of their own horses apparently drowned out all other sound so they didn't notice when Lane's horse stopped running.

Once the four riders were past the gully, Lane reined his horse back into the valley and walked him across the creek and then downstream a way where a small cluster of cottonwoods would hide him and the horse from anyone on the other side of the creek.

It wasn't long till the four horsemen came back, riding slowly. He could tell from the sounds that they were checking every side pocket on that side of the creek. Apparently they were sure that Lane was hiding in some gully over there. They'd soon figure out that he wasn't on that side.

As soon as the riders were past him, going back toward the wagons, Lane put his horse to a trot down the valley, keeping on the far side of the creek from the trail. By the time they discovered he wasn't hiding somewhere in the valley, he hoped to be well on his way to the fort.

Once out of the valley, Lane looked for the main road up by the Platte. It was many wagons wide and the ruts were worn deep. It hadn't been used much since the railroad went through last year, but it would take a lot of time and much effort on Mother Nature's part to erase those tracks.

Turning down the road, Lane put his horse to

an easy lope until he was sure he was far enough away that Widlow's men wouldn't find him. An hour later, he pulled off the road to the edge of the river and found a soft place with good grass where both he and his horse could rest.

He was up at dawn and soon moving down the river. It wasn't long until the fort came into sight and he reined over to a sentry, who asked him to explain his mission. Then he was allowed to pass.

Before he got to headquarters, where he had been directed to go, he was met by a rather heavy man with brown hair and gray eyes who had been watching him intently since he'd first come into sight.

"Came from the west, didn't you?" the man asked.

Lane nodded.

"Seen anything of a wagon train with four wagons?" the brown-haired man asked then.

Lane stared at him, then swung out of the saddle. "What do you know about that train?" he demanded.

"I know it should have been here before this," the man said. "I've got a shipment on that train that I was to meet here at Fort McPherson and take on to Omaha on the cars. It has to be there in less than a week."

"That train is never going to get here," Lane said. "Everybody on the train was murdered."

The man's face turned white. "Everybody?" he choked.

"Everybody but Jud Bumbry. Do you know him?"

The man nodded numbly. "Why?" he asked.

"Robbery, I figure," Lane said. "At least, they tore everything out of the wagons."

"How do you know so much?" the man asked, gaining some control of himself.

"I was a hunter for the train. I was on a hunt when the outlaws struck. My brother was killed." Lane scowled at the man. "Who are you, mister?"

"My name is Henry Gordon. I have a ranch not far from here. But I also own a mine just west of Denver."

Two young ladies came from one of the buildings and hurried to Gordon. The rancher welcomed them and quickly explained that the wagon train had been robbed. "Looks like Robinson has beaten us again," he concluded.

Lane watched the two women, realizing they were little more than girls, especially the younger one, who was under twenty, he guessed. The other one must be twenty or a bit older.

Gordon suddenly seemed to remember Lane. He turned to him. "These are my daughters, Stella and Bessie. You didn't tell me who you were."

"Lane Perry. Tried my luck at mining and didn't make it. My brother, Chris, and I hooked on with

Bumbry's wagon train as hunters in order to get back to Missouri to our farm."

"Sorry to hear about your brother," the older girl said.

Lane nodded and looked the girls over. The older one, Stella, was fixed up pretty plain. Her auburn hair was pulled back like stretched rope and twisted up in a bun on the back of her head. Lane liked her hazel eyes.

The younger girl, Bessie, was anything but plain. She had red hair and she let it bounce down her back. Her blue eyes were the eyes of a flirt if Lane had ever seen any. She was quite a bit smaller than Stella, barely five feet tall, and he was sure she wouldn't weigh more than a hundred pounds.

"The thieves didn't seem to be taking any of the stuff they were dragging out of the wagons," Lane volunteered.

"I have to find out if my shipment is there," Gordon said.

"I doubt if anything of value will be left, the way they were pawing over things," Lane said.

"It won't be that easy to find," Gordon said. "Will you take me out there?"

"I'm on my way to talk to the commander of the fort," Lane said. "I think this is a job for the soldiers."

"I'm going out there," Gordon said emphatically.

Gordon fell into step with Lane as Lane headed for the post headquarters. The officer of the day listened to Lane's report, then relayed it to the post commander. He was back in a few minutes.

"Sergeant Dodson with a squad of three men will accompany you back to the massacre site," the officer said. "If possible, they will find out who the perpetrators were and where they went."

Lane knew he couldn't expect any more. He was sure the colonel didn't fully believe him or he would have sent a wagon to bring back the bodies and at least twenty men just in case Widlow and his gang were still there. A sergeant and three privates would hardly be a match for Widlow's crew.

"We must get out there immediately," Gordon said as they left the headquarters.

Lane didn't say anything, but he was as eager to get back there as Gordon was. They found the two Gordon girls waiting where they had left them.

"When do we start?" Stella Gordon asked.

Lane looked at her in disbelief. "This is no trip for women," he said.

Stella looked at Lane steadily. "I do much of my father's business," she said quietly. "I'm going to see what happened to our shipment."

Lane stared at her. The statement was the kind that left no room for argument. Yet a woman should definitely not go on this mission. He turned to Henry Gordon.

"Are you going to let her go?" Lane asked.

Gordon shook his head. "Her mother died when she was twelve and Bessie was nine. She's been the lady of the house ever since. I don't have any better luck bossing her around than I did her mother. And she is right. She does help me a great deal with my business."

"But that was a massacre out there," Lane argued. "And four men were murdered. Those murderers might still be there."

"We'll have a soldier escort," Stella said. "They won't tackle an army patrol."

"It will be fun," Bessie added. "All those soldiers!"

Lane felt that his first impression of Bessie was being supported. Bessie was not thinking of the murdered men, nor of the danger to anyone going into that area where the murderers might be, but of the soldiers who were going. A lot of men for her to toy with. He frowned as it flashed across his mind that he wouldn't mind being one of those men. She was about the prettiest girl he'd ever seen.

A sergeant came striding toward them. Lane guessed him to be a little older than he was, perhaps twenty-five. With his ramrod-straight back and flashing eyes, he looked neat even in his field uniform.

"I'm Sergeant Ted Dodson," he said crisply. "My three men are preparing for detail. They'll be here in a few minutes. Do you gentlemen have horses?"

"I have a tired one," Lane said.

"I don't have a horse," Gordon said. "I'm Hank Gordon. We came from Denver by stage to Julesburg and on the train here. These are my daughters, Stella and Bessie. They don't have horses, either."

Dodson's eyes popped. "Are they going?"

Gordon nodded. "They should have a tent, too."

"By all means—if they're going," Dodson said. "I'll get what is needed."

In less than half an hour, the soldier detail was ready and the Gordons were mounted on army horses. Lane was still riding the horse he had taken from Widlow's line. With a good feed and watering, the animal was ready for the trail, but Lane doubted if he would last long if they had to make a run for it.

He didn't expect any trouble. The murderers would surely be gone when they got there. The soldiers and Gordon would search the remains of the wreck, then come back.

Sergeant Dodson had detailed Lane to lead the way since he was the only one who knew where the site was. Lane wasn't sure he could pick the right valley. But he recalled the tiny creek in the valley. That would help.

Hank Gordon came up to ride beside Lane while the sergeant dropped back to ride with his men and the two Gordon girls.

"Since you're involved in this massacre, you should know why this is so important to me," Gordon said. "As I told you, I own a ranch along the Platte near here. That's why I chose Fort McPherson for delivery of my shipment. I also own a mine in the mountains west of Denver. The ranch was in bad shape, and I mortgaged it for all it was worth. Actually all I really have title to is the cattle. The size of your ranch here is whatever you can keep the other fellow from using.

"I decided to try my hand at mining. A banker in Omaha, Atley Robinson, staked me for the venture, but he took a mortgage on all my stock and also on any mine that I might acquire. That seemed safe enough to me. I was losing my cattle, anyway. So if I didn't strike gold, I was no worse off. If I did hit it rich, I could pay off the bank and have both the mine and the ranch."

"Sounds good," Lane said, trying to see how this affected the current situation. "Did you hit it rich?"

Gordon nodded. "I have a fine claim out there. Making a lot of money. But I tried twice to send gold to the bank in Omaha to pay off my mortgage. Both times the stage was held up before it got to Julesburg and the gold was lost."

Lane nodded. “And you have a deadline to get that money to the bank?”

“Exactly. And that is less than a week away. I know somebody was watching and robbing the stages with my gold. I think Robinson is in on it. He wrote me a letter saying I must have that money in his bank on the due date or he’ll foreclose on the ranch and the mine. That mine is worth many times what the mortgage is. Robinson will be a rich man if I don’t get that mortgage money to him.”

“Sounds like he’s doing what he can to keep you from paying him.”

“That’s how I figure it. I was so sure he had somebody watching the stages that I hit on this plan to get the gold through. Nobody would suspect a small train of disgruntled miners heading home to be carrying gold. I was to meet them here at Fort McPherson where nobody would be watching me or the train. I’d take the gold on into Omaha. Robinson couldn’t refuse to take the money there.”

“Do you suspect Robinson of staging this robbery and murder?”

“I don’t know,” Gordon said. “It looks suspicious. But there is no way Robinson could have known about this shipment.”

“Couldn’t somebody on the train have told him?”

“Nobody knew. Only my mine foreman, who

took care of everything, knew about it and he stayed back at the mine."

Anger surged up in Lane. "Then you are responsible for the deaths of some good men."

Gordon frowned. "How do you figure that? I didn't rob those wagons."

"If Chris and I had known there was a secret shipment of gold in those wagons, we wouldn't have joined the outfit."

Gordon nodded. "If I'd let it be known that there was a gold shipment, I know it would never have gotten through. There was just no way they could have known. Likely this was just a chance robbery."

"Jud Bumbry was in on it," Lane said grimly. "He was the leader of the train and he survived. In fact, he joined in with the gang trying to find me and eliminate the last witness."

"Bumbry must be a traitor," Gordon agreed. "But there is no way he could have known about the gold."

"They were tearing everything out of the wagons and looking for something," Lane said.

"But it's impossible," Gordon said in disbelief. "I made sure nobody on that train had any idea about the gold. My worry was to get them to let me have my gold when they got to Fort McPherson with it."

"You don't have that worry now," Lane said. "And I don't have a brother."

"I'm extremely sorry about your brother," Gordon said. "But there is just no way my gold could have been responsible for his death."

Lane had to believe he was sincere in thinking that. But it still nagged him that Bumbry and Widlow knew there was something valuable in those wagons.

Gordon dropped back and soon the sergeant came forward to ride beside Lane.

"We've come quite a ways," Dodson said. "Are you sure you'll know the valley when you see it?"

Lane nodded. "I think so. There are a lot of valleys, but not many with creeks. There was a tiny creek in this one."

They came to a dip in the trail with a small stream running through it. Hundreds of wagons crossing it had cut the banks of the little stream into a muddy bog, but evidently the ground underneath was solid enough that it had not become a major problem.

Lane looked to the south. That tiny stream came from the valley and he saw small willows and cottonwoods here and there along the water. That had to be it, he decided.

He led the caravan up the stream and into the valley. Nothing looked familiar to Lane, but then he had come down that valley in the dark last night. Only when he approached the bend in the valley was he sure that this was the right one.

Around the corner, they came in sight of the wagons. Lane wouldn't have been surprised to find the outlaws still there. But the scene was quiet. Sergeant Dodson held up his hand.

"Mr. Gordon, you and your daughters stay back till we see what lies ahead."

"I want to see those wagons," Gordon said.

"You'll get your chance. But we have a burial detail to carry out first."

"Should have brought a wagon to take the bodies back to the fort," Lane said.

"I suggested it," Dodson said. "But they didn't really believe your story about a massacre, I'm afraid. So we'll bury the bodies as best we can and have a detail come out later with coffins and exhume them and bring them in for proper burial."

That wasn't what Lane wanted for his brother, but circumstances seemed to dictate that it was the way things were going to be.

Lane found his brother close to one of the wagons. There was no sign that his death had been anything but quick. Grief cut through him like a knife. While Lane lingered there, Sergeant Dodson detailed his three privates to dig a mass grave for the four men. Lane could see Gordon fretting back where the sergeant had left him. If it had not been for the girls, Lane was sure that Gordon would have been up here examining these wagons right now.

When the privates had wrapped the bodies in blankets found near the wagons and carried them to the grave they had dug, the sergeant motioned for Gordon and his daughters to come over.

Lane turned his attention to the wagons then, too. There was nothing more he could do for his brother. The contents of the wagons were scattered over the grass. Most of the things were possessions of the men making the trip back to their original homes. Pots, pans, bedding, small stoves, shovels, even a couple of rifles were scattered around. There were some satchels of clothes that had been ripped open, but no gold.

Lane kept a close eye on Hank Gordon. Only he knew where the gold was hidden in these wagons. Lane expected to see him pawing through some of the things. But he merely walked around, examining some wagon boxes and wagon frames. Two of the wagons had the bottoms of the boxes torn out. Lane couldn't see that Gordon showed any real excitement as he had when he'd been trying to get out here.

Lane was on the point of asking him about his gold when a rifle roared from up the valley. He wheeled that way. Five riders were galloping down toward them from the top of the hill. Lane knew it was the same men who had ambushed the wagons. Now they were set on another massacre.

IV

"Take cover!" Sergeant Dodson shouted.

The privates dropped down and began to return the fire. The horsemen roaring down from the top of the valley suddenly reined up and threw themselves out of their saddles.

Lane dropped down behind a shattered wagon box and prepared to make a good account of himself. Having the four soldiers along gave him confidence. The outlaws would not find a few helpless men as they had when they had surprised the wagon train.

The soldiers were making plenty of racket with their rifles. Lane looked for Stella and Bessie. It wasn't likely the outlaws would fire at them, but they could be hit easily enough by the wild shots that were flying back and forth. He was surprised to see Stella behind another wagon, using a rifle as if she'd done it all her life. Judging from what he'd seen of her so far, maybe she had. Bessie was flat on the ground next to her, obviously badly frightened.

Lane fired at any target he saw, then reloaded his gun. Moving quickly, he crossed to the wagon where the girls were. They were more exposed than some of the men.

"Need any help?" Lane asked, dropping down beside the pair.

"They're not coming any closer," Stella said. "There aren't any more of them than there are of us. Who are they, anyway?"

"Same bunch that murdered these men with the wagons," Lane said.

"I'm glad you came over to help us," Bessie said, her teeth chattering. "We were all alone over here."

Lane glanced at Stella. "You aren't helpless as long as she can handle a rifle like that."

"Pa always said if you're going to live where guns are used, you'd better be able to use them," Stella said.

"I—I'm afraid of guns," Bessie said.

Lane fired again, but he realized those men were almost out of range of his revolver. But they weren't out of range of the rifles of Stella and the soldiers. The raiders soon broke for their horses and, swinging into the saddles, kicked their animals into a gallop.

"Guess we didn't get any of them," one soldier said disgustedly.

"One horse ran off without a rider," Sergeant Dodson said. "Anybody here hit?"

It was then that Lane saw Hank Gordon off to one side where he'd been looking at the last wagon when the attack had started. Gordon was flat on the ground. He'd obviously been hit.

Lane was the first to reach the fallen rancher. Before he turned him over, he knew the verdict.

When he did turn him, the blue-rimmed hole in the middle of his forehead told the whole story. Evidently he had been hit by the first volley.

Lane turned away. He should say something to comfort the two Gordon girls, but he couldn't think of anything decent to say. The soldiers all made an effort to comfort them, but it was useless until the initial shock of their grief wore off.

Sergeant Dodson, as the official leader of the detail, took over. Lane expected him to order them all back to the fort. But he detailed Private Ray Lyon to take the body back to the fort and escort the girls there.

"Aren't you going?" Stella asked.

"Not as long as there is a chance we can get those outlaws. With one empty saddle in their outfit, there are only four of them left. And there will be four of us, counting Lane." He looked at Lane. "Do you figure on staying?"

"I'll stay whether you do or not," Lane said.

"We're staying, too," Stella said.

Lane frowned. "You can't. You saw what kind of men these are. We're going to try to capture them and bring them to justice."

"I'll help," Stella said firmly, in spite of the tears running down her face. "Bessie and I have to finish the job our father started. We're going to get that gold to the bank in time to save our ranch and mine. Those are ours now that Pa is dead."

"Didn't the outlaws get the gold?" Lane asked.

"Not according to Pa. I was with him examining the wagons just before the shooting started. Then I came over to Bessie and that's when they made the attack."

"Did your pa say that the outlaws didn't get the gold?"

"He said it was still here with the wagons." Stella bit her lip. "But he didn't say where it is hidden."

Lane realized that Widlow probably hadn't found the gold. If he had, he would have been gone long before this. He and his men were obviously still hoping to find it. He could hardly fathom a girl as strong-willed and apparently as fearless as Stella. He looked across at Bessie. Even in her sorrow, she was as pretty as a canyon sunset.

"You'll go back to the fort, won't you?" Lane said.

Bessie looked around. Then she shook her head. "Stella and I stay together." Her eyes flitted from Lane to the soldiers and back to Lane. "I'll be safe with all these men around."

Lane frowned. But he didn't say any more. Nobody was going to change Stella's mind. If she thought Bessie should go back to the fort, she would say so.

"We'll be back at the fort in time for the funeral," Stella said. "Right now our work is here."

Hank Gordon's body was tied onto a saddle and Private Lyon given final instructions from the sergeant. "Tell them to send out four coffins and get these other bodies," he said. "Maybe they'll believe you now that you're an eyewitness."

Once the private had started away with Gordon's body, Sergeant Dodson turned up the valley. "Let's see if we can find the outlaw who didn't ride out," he said.

Lane fell in step with him and they moved cautiously upward, guns in their hands. A wounded outlaw could be as dangerous as a wounded rattlesnake.

They found the man close to where his horse had been. At first, Lane thought he was dead. But when they got close, he saw he was breathing. Then he saw the furrow cut in his scalp. A bullet had creased him and knocked him out but likely had done no permanent damage.

The sergeant took out his canteen. "I'll douse him with water. You hold your gun on him. If he wants to fight, kill him. If he lives, I'm going to take him in to stand trial. He may not be the man who killed Gordon, but I'll charge him with the murder, anyway."

Lane followed instructions. The cold splash of water roused the outlaw and in a couple of minutes he was trying to sit up. He looked at Sergeant Dodson, then at Lane's gun, and his eyes grew wider.

"Who are you?" Dodson demanded.

"Who are *you?*" the outlaw retorted. "And where's my buddies?"

"They ran off and left you to face the music by yourself," Dodson said. "And you'll swing higher than a kite, too."

The color drained out of the man's face. "Easy said he'd never leave one of us."

"Who is Easy?" Dodson asked.

The man looked around wildly and Lane tightened his grip on the gun. "If I tell you all I know, maybe you'll let me go?" he said.

"Maybe," Dodson said.

"My name is Fel Turley. Easy Widlow is my boss. We've been working this entire area. I don't know who hired Easy to hit this wagon train, but we was to get half the gold if we did."

"What gold?" Lane demanded.

Turley shrugged. "I don't know. There was supposed to be a shipment of gold in those wagons."

"And you didn't find it?" Dodson said.

"There ain't no gold in them wagons," Turley said. "We tore them all to pieces and there just ain't no gold there. Easy and this traitor who helped us take the wagons, Bumbry, still say it's there and we're going to find it."

"How did you get the idea there was gold there?" Lane demanded.

"I told you I don't know. I just do what I'm

told. It wasn't my idea to kill everybody, but that was our orders."

"Who gave those orders?" Lane asked.

Turley cringed at the question. "It wasn't me. And it wasn't Easy. It was the turncoat, Bumbry. He didn't want anybody left who could recognize him."

Lane was sure Turley was telling the truth as far as he knew it. Jud Bumbry was to blame for this massacre.

But the sergeant wasn't satisfied. "Apparently your leader went along with the idea."

Turley nodded. "He ain't too anxious to leave witnesses, either."

Those two were birds of a feather, Lane guessed. Jud Bumbry knew that he would be blamed because everyone in the wagon train had objected to turning off the main trail to make the delivery Bumbry said he had to make up here. If any of those drivers had lived, he would surely have set the law on Bumbry for leading them into this trap. From what Lane had heard of Easy Widlow, that outlaw wouldn't turn a hair at murder, either, if he could see any personal advantage in it. In this case, if Lane hadn't escaped, there would have been no clue that would have pointed to him and his gang.

Dodson got Turley to his feet and made him walk over to the wagons. There he posted his two privates, Pud Krause and Oliver Voage, to guard him, after informing Turley that he'd be taken to Fort McPherson and tried for murder. Turley yelled that it wasn't fair after he'd told all he knew.

Bessie had been virtually clinging to Pud Krause and he didn't seem to mind at all. But now that Lane and the sergeant were back with the prisoner, she turned her attention to Lane.

"Let's help Stella look for Pa's gold," she suggested.

Lane couldn't argue with that idea. The sooner they found the gold, the quicker they could get the girls out of this valley. As long as they stayed here, there was great danger from Easy Widlow and his gang. According to Fel Turley, Widlow and Bumbry were convinced the gold was still here. They'd make every effort to get it.

"Just where are you looking for the gold?" Lane asked Stella.

"Everywhere," she said. "Pa didn't tell me where his foreman put it, but he said nobody would find it."

"Apparently, he was right about that. How much is there?"

"About seven or eight pounds," Stella said. "That will pay off the mortgage."

"That would take a big hiding place," Lane said. "But I don't see any place where it could be that those thieves haven't looked."

"Maybe they found it," Bessie said.

"Turley didn't think so," Lane said. "But if Bumbry or Widlow found the gold, they might have decided to divide it between the two of them and let the rest of the gang think the loot had not been found."

Lane could see that Stella didn't think so and he was hoping she was right. Getting that mortgage paid off meant everything to the two girls, and Lane shared their hope that they could keep the mine and the ranch.

"Pa said it was still here," Stella said. "He told me that just before the shooting started. So it's here. Just where is the question."

"You don't have long to pay off that mortgage, either, according to what your pa told me," Lane said.

"Less than a week," Stella agreed. "We should have met the wagons near Julesburg and taken it from there on the train. But Pa was sure the wagons would get to Fort McPherson in plenty of time and we'd take the train in from here."

"If we'd met it at Julesburg, we could have avoided this holdup," Bessie said.

"I doubt that," Lane said. "If Bumbry knew someone would meet the wagons at Julesburg, he'd have staged the holdup somewhere before they got to Julesburg."

"Let's keep looking," Stella said. "Maybe he hid some of it in the rims of the wheels. I've heard of things being hidden in hollowed-out rims."

"Not eight pounds of gold," Lane said.

"Where else could it be?" Bessie asked. "They've torn up the wagon boxes. There were no secret places there—unless they found it."

"You know they didn't," Stella said sternly, "because Pa said they didn't. Let's each one go over a wagon. It may be in small packages in several places."

That made sense to Lane. He turned toward the wagon nearest the top of the valley. The floor had been ripped up. There was no concealed pocket anywhere. He checked the boards that had been torn off the sides of the box. Then he checked the wheels, thinking of the hollowed-out rims. But there was no sign that any wheel had been tampered with.

This wagon had been hit several times in the shooting. He had no way of knowing whether those bullet holes had been made during the massacre or in the attack today. It made no difference.

He saw where a bullet had glanced off an axle. It had dug into the wood a quarter of an inch before ricocheting off into the air. That didn't interest him, but something about the groove dug into the wood did. There seemed to be a crack right where the bullet had struck. No bullet should crack a piece of wood as strong as a wagon axle.

Bending close, Lane examined the axle. Only then did he see that the axle had been cut with a saw lengthwise. Looking on the side of the axle, he saw the big nails that were holding the axle together, probably just as stout as it was before it had been sawed down the middle.

Lane called the girls over. Sergeant Dodson came, too. He pointed out what he had found.

"My guess is the gold is in this axle. That axle is wide enough that a hollowed-out spot could be made to hide the stuff. And it wouldn't weaken the axle much."

"How are we going to split the axle to see?" Stella asked, excitement in her face.

"Let me see if I can find something in all this stuff they have dumped on the ground," Dodson said. "There must be something we can use to pry open that axle."

Lane went with him to search and found an iron bar with one end pounded out to a sharp edge. Bringing it back to the axle, he and Dodson forced it into the tiny crack in the wood.

The nails held firmly at first and squealed like animals in pain when they were forced to yield. Finally the axle came in two. Lane stared. There were four pockets hollowed out of the hardwood. In each pocket was a pouch. He stooped and picked up one. It was amazingly heavy for its size. He handed it to Stella.

With trembling fingers, she opened it. No one

was surprised when gold dust was revealed. Lane estimated there must be close to two pounds in that pouch. The other three looked about the same size.

"We'll get this to Fort McPherson as quickly as possible and Bessie and I will catch the train to Omaha," Stella said. "Pa said no outlaws would find it and he was right."

"Almost kept us from finding it, too," Lane said.

Sergeant Dodson glanced at the sun sinking low in the west. "We can't make it back to the fort tonight. Let's go down the valley a ways to get away from these wagons and camp. We'll go in early tomorrow."

"We could ride in the dark," Stella suggested.

"We'd be sitting ducks for those killers," Dodson argued. "You can bet they'll watch us. If we start off for the fort tonight, they'll be sure that we have found the gold and they'll hit us to get it."

Reluctantly, Stella agreed to spend the night in the valley. Dodson chose a site some distance away from the wagons. He detailed a soldier to set up the tent for the girls. Pud Krause leaped forward to volunteer for the chore. Lane could see that he had his eye on Bessie. A twinge of jealousy swept over him, but Lane put it aside. Bessie was very pretty and she obviously liked Lane. But she liked every man who was within her sight.

Lane was eager to get the girls and their gold to Fort McPherson, but he wasn't as eager to go there himself. His brother had been murdered. He knew the ones responsible for that murder and he found it hard to turn his back on a chance to bring them to justice, one way or another.

They had barely settled into their new camp when Voage, standing guard, signaled that someone was coming. Lane grabbed his rifle from his saddle boot, but his alarm faded some when he saw that Voage was pointing down the valley.

Within a minute, Voage signaled it was safe and Private Ray Lyon, who had been detailed to take Hank Gordon's body back to the fort, came into view. There was a man with him.

"This is Atley Robinson," Lyon announced. "He was coming up here looking for Henry Gordon and his daughters. He had a small escort, so I sent them back with the body and I brought Mr. Robinson up here."

Lane sized up the man. So this was the Omaha banker that Henry Gordon had said held the mortgage that must be paid off within a week. Robinson was a tall man and overweight. He sat in his saddle like a loosely tied sack of grain.

This was going to make it easy for Stella and Bessie. They could pay off the banker right now and not even have to go on to Omaha. He saw that Stella had the same idea. Just as soon as the formal introductions had been made, she told

Robinson that she had the gold so she'd pay off the mortgage right now.

The banker held up his hand. "I can't do that," he said, his florid face trying to look sad. But Lane was sure he saw a gleam in his muddy brown eyes. "That contract says it must be paid at the bank by July first. If you don't have the money there by that date, you'll forfeit everything according to the contract."

V

Lane stared in disbelief at the banker. The late-afternoon sun was glinting off a large stone in the ring on Robinson's hand. Lane doubted if it was a diamond because of its size, but he couldn't be sure. It was appropriate because everything about Atley Robinson was big. But there was nothing big about his heart. He could see the fury building in Stella.

"Look," she said, her voice choking. "I'm offering you the money to pay off that mortgage. You have to take it."

Robinson shook his head. "Oh, no, I don't. The contract your father signed says that all transactions concerning this mortgage must take place in my office in the bank."

Lane pushed up to face the banker, nose to nose. "What's your real reason for not taking the money?" he demanded.

Robinson backed off a couple of steps. "You heard my reason. It's in the contract. Besides, if I took that gold and started back to civilization with it, those robbers who are trying to get it would jump on me instantly."

Lane had to agree that the banker was probably thinking straight on that. Suddenly a new thought hit him. Robinson had been in camp only a few minutes. Nobody had mentioned the robbery.

"How did you know there were robbers around?"

A startled look flashed across the banker's face. Then a condescending glare took its place. "The soldier who guided me here said it was the robbers who killed Henry Gordon."

Lane had to admit that was likely the truth, too, but he couldn't forget that startled look on the banker's face when Lane first asked him the question. Then Stella put words to another thought in Lane's mind.

"You don't want to take the gold now because you're hoping I won't get it to your bank on time and you can foreclose on the mine. You know that mine is worth many times what the mortgage is."

"You're crazy," Robinson said. "You've got a much better chance of getting that gold through with your soldier escort."

"You can stay here tonight and ride back to the fort with us tomorrow," Lane suggested. "Then you'd have the benefit of the soldier escort, too."

Robinson scowled. "Won't make any difference. The transaction has to be made in my office in Omaha."

"You're the lowest kind of thief," Lane snapped, his fists clenched. "When are you leaving?"

Robinson backed off a couple of more steps.

"It's getting late. I can't make it very far before dark. I'll accept the invitation to stay here in your camp till morning."

"Only on one condition," Lane snapped. "That you take this gold and cancel that mortgage."

"I can't do that," Robinson said. "The contract—"

Lane jerked his gun out of his holster. "Then I'll give you just one minute to get out of this camp. After that, I start shooting."

Robinson's face blanched and he backed toward his horse. Lane shot a glance at Sergeant Dodson. He was in charge of this camp. He could overrule Lane with just a word. But the sergeant was glaring at Robinson and making no move to counteract Lane's ultimatum.

Robinson looked over at Dodson and apparently didn't see anything to encourage him to stay. He wheeled and climbed laboriously into the saddle. When he jerked the reins tight and turned to glare at Lane, Lane lifted his gun another inch. It was all the banker needed. He kicked his horse into a jolting trot and headed toward the river.

Suddenly he jerked up on the reins. Twisting in the saddle, he shouted at the sergeant, "Don't you have to furnish me with an escort?"

"All I'll furnish you is an extra prod to get you out of here," Dodson yelled back. "Even a dummy can't get lost between here and the fort. Ride to the river, then turn downstream."

Robinson wheeled back and nudged his horse onward.

Lane turned to the sergeant. "Thanks for backing me up."

"You're right about him," Dodson said. "He's a bigger thief than Easy Widlow. He just pretends to be legal about it."

The camp settled down, but shortly after dark, Private Voage called another warning. A rider was approaching. Unable to see who it was, Lane prepared for an attack from Widlow. He might think a night attack would conquer them. By now, he may have concluded that they had found the gold or they wouldn't have moved away from the wagons.

Running down the valley where Voage was stationed, Lane waited for the rider to come in. The newcomer didn't seem to be trying to keep quiet. Either he was not one of Widlow's men or he was a decoy to cover up an attack from some other point.

Then the man was close enough for Lane to see him in the gloom. He was no one Lane had ever seen before. Maybe he was one of Widlow's men. Stella was beside Lane now, holding a rifle ready to shoot.

"What are you doing here?" she demanded of the rider.

"Do you know him?" Lane asked.

"He's Ken Sanford, our mine foreman," Stella

said. Turning her attention back to the rider, she glared at him. "You're a long way from your job, Ken."

"I've been worried about that gold shipment," he said. "The mine can get along without me for a few days. I knew your pa was going to move the shipment from the wagons to the train at Fort McPherson. I thought he might need help."

"How did you find us out here?" Lane demanded.

"Followed that fat banker and his escort till he switched to the one soldier. Had no trouble following them."

"Did you see the banker going back?" Stella asked.

Sanford hesitated. "Well, I saw some rider come my way. I got out of sight just in case he was someone I didn't want to see."

"We're glad you came," Bessie said. "We need all the help we can get."

Lane noticed that Stella was not extending the welcome that her sister was. He watched her as she looked at the mine foreman in the dying firelight.

"If you're going to stay with us, you'll have to make arrangements with Sergeant Dodson," Stella said.

"I assume there is some trouble here," Sanford said.

"You're on the right track," Lane said.

He watched the man move over to Sergeant Dodson, who had gone back to the fire when he discovered that the girls knew the visitor. After Sanford was gone, Lane turned to Stella.

"You don't seem very happy to see your mine foreman," he said.

"There just isn't any legitimate reason for his being here," she said.

"He said he was worried about Pa," Bessie said. "I wish he'd gotten here in time to save Pa."

Stella didn't seem swayed by Bessie's loyalty. "I'm not sure how much help that would have been," she said.

"You're always suspicious of everyone," Bessie snapped. "If you just trusted people more, you'd have a lot more friends."

Lane stayed out of the argument, but he wondered if Bessie was right. Stella didn't repulse friends, he decided; she just made sure they were friendly before she extended her own friendship. There was no question that Bessie had extended her friendship to Lane, but he still wasn't sure about Stella. She was reserved around everyone.

"Do you have reason to question Sanford's motives?" Lane asked.

"Plenty," Stella said. "Ken was the only man that Pa trusted. He was the one who hid the gold in the wagons."

Lane looked over to the spot where Sanford was talking to Sergeant Dodson. "Do you think he told someone?"

"How else did they know there was gold in those wagons?" Stella snapped.

"They didn't know where it was."

"Maybe Ken kept that to himself." Stella frowned as she stared at the mine foreman talking to the sergeant. "If he'd told them where it was, it would have been gone when he got here. But if they had taken possession of the wagons but hadn't found the gold, then he could cut himself in on it."

"What are we going to do with the gold?" Bessie asked Stella.

"Get it to the bank in Omaha," Stella said firmly.

"What if we can't?" Bessie said, worry on her face. "That banker seemed more interested in foreclosing than in getting his money."

"He is," Stella agreed. "But that doesn't mean we can't make him take the gold and tear up the mortgage."

"I don't think he'll ever let us get to Omaha with it," Bessie said. "I think we should split up the gold and use it ourselves. That's better than losing everything."

"We're not going to lose everything," Stella said angrily. "We're going to save our mine and the ranch."

"Let me keep half and you half," Bessie suggested.

Stella shook her head. "Somebody would get it away from you. I'm the oldest. I'll keep it."

Lane felt that he should be somewhere else. He wanted no part of a family quarrel. That gold did belong as much to Bessie as it did to Stella, but he had to agree that Stella was much more likely to hang on to it than Bessie was. Stella was all business; Bessie was anything but business.

Lane moved away and Bessie soon followed. "It isn't fair," she said softly to him. "I have as much right to that gold as she has."

"She's trying to save it to pay off Robinson," Lane said, more to soothe Bessie's feelings than to justify Stella. He felt that he could see Bessie's side of it, but sound reason told him the gold was safer in Stella's hands. Still, he found it hard to reason with Bessie. She was beautiful and, when she ran her fingers along his arm, he could feel his resistance to her arguments melting away.

"If we each had half," Bessie said, "we'd lose only half if someone did steal what one of us had. But if Stella keeps it and someone steals it from her, he'll get it all."

Lane nodded. That might make sense, but he knew how easily some thief could talk Bessie out of it. No thief would get it that easily from Stella.

"Are you asking me to help you talk Stella into giving you half of the gold?" he asked.

"It is half mine, isn't it?" Bessie said.

"Of course. And I think Stella will see to it you get your share of the ranch and the mine she's trying to save. I'm sorry, Bessie, but I don't want to get involved in a family quarrel. I do want to see you two keep your property."

"I only want what is mine," Bessie said. Her fingers crept up to his shoulder. "Please. I need help."

Lane swallowed hard. Bessie could easily wrap him around her finger if he would allow it. And he would revel in allowing it, but he knew that the gold was safer in Stella's hands.

"I can't do it, Bessie. That gold belongs to both of you girls. If I thought Stella was intending to keep it all, I'd help you. But I really think she will share with you."

Bessie gave a sigh of resignation and turned away to walk to the edge of the firelight. Lane watched to make sure she didn't go too far. It could be dangerous beyond the circle of light.

Lane noticed that Sanford had apparently made arrangements with Sergeant Dodson to spend the night in camp. Wandering around before hitting his blankets, Lane noticed that Bessie was out at the perimeter of the camp talking to one of the privates, Pud Krause. Krause had shown more interest in Bessie than any of the soldiers. Lane wondered idly if she was trying to get him to help her persuade Stella to give her custody of half of the gold. Lane couldn't see why that was so important since all the gold was destined to go to the Omaha bank to pay off the mortgage on the ranch and mine.

Finding his bedroll, Lane saw that Stella had already gone to her tent. Bessie soon joined her. Then Lane dropped off to sleep.

He was jarred out of his sleep by a scream. His first thought was that Widlow's men were attacking. Then his mind cleared enough to realize that the scream hadn't been the guard calling out an alarm. It had originated right here in the camp. Lane was on his feet almost instantly. In another second he was running toward the tent where the scream was repeated.

Before he reached it, both girls, clad in long nightgowns, exploded out of the tent with a man hanging on to Stella. Lane didn't stop to identify the man but lunged at him, slamming a fist into his middle, knocking him away from the girl.

The man fought back, but the fury in Lane blinded him to pain and he smashed at the man with both fists, knocking him down. The man scrambled to his feet. But before he got straightened up, Lane was after him again. His fist to the face did straighten him up and sent him reeling backward.

It was only then that he got a look at the other man's face and recognized Ken Sanford, the mine foreman. Why he had been in the tent was neither clear nor important to Lane right then. The fact that he had been there was all that he needed to send him after Sanford with a fury that nothing, certainly not Sanford, could stop.

Lane's next blow flattened Sanford. When he got up, Lane flattened him again. This time Sanford didn't try to get up. It was all Lane could do to keep from kicking him in the ribs. No punishment could be too severe, he thought.

Grabbing Sanford by the shirt front, he dragged him to his feet. By this time Dodson and both girls were right behind Lane.

"What were you up to?" Lane demanded.

"He was after the gold," Stella said. Her voice was almost calm. "Grabbed me when I was asleep. Threatened to kill me if I yelled. Had a hand over my mouth and demanded to know where I hid the gold. Bessie screamed."

"We ought to string him up," Pud Krause put in. He had come over from his guard post and was standing at Bessie's side as if to protect her.

"You didn't tell him, did you?" Lane asked, turning to look at Stella.

"Of course not," Stella said. "But this proves that he's the one who was really behind this massacre."

Krause suddenly yelled and Lane wheeled to look at the private. He was staring past Lane, and

Lane spun back. Sanford was running like a quail seeking cover.

"Shoot him," the sergeant yelled. He was without his gun. The private seemed to have forgotten he had his rifle in his hand. In his haste, Lane had left his own gun in his bedroll. Ken Sanford escaped into the darkness.

"Think he'll go back to Denver?" Lane asked.

"He'll probably join the gang that's trying to get the gold," Stella said. "Obviously he knows Jud Bumbry. He must have been the one who told Bumbry about the gold in the wagons."

Dodson ordered Krause back to his sentry post, then helped Bessie straighten up the tent. Lane turned his attention to Stella.

"You have to hide that gold. Sanford might try again to steal it."

"I'll split it up and hide it in several places. If he should find some, he won't get it all."

"Good idea," Lane agreed. He went over to the rock where Fel Turley, the outlaw they had captured, was lying, bound. "How many men are with Widlow now?"

"Enough to wipe you out," Turley growled. "He's got Medder and Copo and Bumbry. And maybe this fellow you just let get away."

As much as Lane wanted to even the score with Bumbry and Widlow, he knew his immediate task was to get the girls back to Fort McPherson with their gold. He really didn't expect Sanford to make another attempt tonight to steal the pouches. He couldn't hope to get away as easily again as he had this time.

It was barely dawn when Lane was brought out of his blankets again by a yell from Stella. Lane was on his feet in an instant and this time he had his gun in his hand.

He found Stella in front of the tent, alarm in her face. "Bessie is gone," she cried.

"How could she get away without you knowing it?"

"I don't know. But she's gone."

"Do you think Sanford kidnapped her?"

Stella shook her head. "I'd surely have heard him because Bessie would have fought back. She must have slipped out on her own."

"Is your gold safe?" Lane asked.

Stella made a quick survey of several spots inside the tent and close by outside. "One bag is gone," she said. "The other three are all right."

The sergeant came over, awakened by Stella's yell.

Lane turned to him. "Are all your men here?"

Dodson's eyes flipped over Stella and Lane. "I'll see."

In a couple of minutes, the sergeant was back. "Private Krause is missing from his guard post. Do you suppose the outlaws could have slipped up and kidnapped him?"

Lane shook his head. “I’m afraid he has deserted—along with Stella’s sister and some of the gold.”

“Oh, she wouldn’t!” Stella said. She stared at Lane. “She would, wouldn’t she?” she added softly.

VI

Bessie hadn't found it easy to slip out of the tent without waking Stella. If Stella woke up, she'd demand an explanation and Bessie hadn't been able to think of a logical one.

Once outside, she slipped around behind the tent where she had seen Stella moving a small rock. Bessie had guessed that Stella was hiding the gold. After Ken Sanford had come so close to getting it, Stella would almost certainly do something to protect it from another robbery attempt.

When Bessie moved the rock, she found a small pouch and she knew it was the gold. But this was not all of it. In fact, this was only a fourth of it. There had been four pouches and all seemed to be about the same size. She should have at least two of the pouches to get her share.

Stella would say she was stealing it, but she wasn't. If she could find all four pouches, she'd take the gold to Fort McPherson somehow and either take it or send it to the Omaha bank where it would pay off the mortgage. If she let Stella handle it, the gold would go when the soldiers went to the fort. It would be a dead giveaway to the outlaws that the gold was there. They'd start a battle and somehow they'd get the gold. The only way to be sure to get it to the train was to sneak it away when nobody expected it.

Although Bessie looked in a dozen different places, she couldn't find any more pouches of gold. Maybe Stella had them in the tent. She didn't dare go back in there looking for them. She was still rummaging around when Pud Krause came back from his guard post.

"I thought I saw you leave the tent," he whispered. "Why didn't you come over?"

"I've been trying to find all the gold," Bessie whispered. "I just found one pouch."

"I'll help you hunt," Krause said.

Five minutes of poking around as silently as shadows failed to turn up any more of the pouches. Stella turned over inside the tent. And close to the dying embers of the supper fire, Sergeant Dodson switched sides.

"We've got to get out of here," Krause whispered. "Let's take what we've got and go."

Bessie wasn't in favor of that. Her purpose was either to get her share of the gold and protect it or get it all and take it to the train before the outlaws suspected what was going on. One pouch of gold wouldn't be enough. But maybe it would save that much because she was convinced that whatever stayed here would be stolen by the robbers.

Gripping the little pouch, she followed the private to the picketed horses. Quietly Krause saddled his and Bessie's horses. Bessie kept an eye on the camp, wondering if they could get away without being caught.

She kept wishing she could have convinced Lane Perry to help her. She had more faith in Lane than she did in Pud Krause. But the private was easier to wrap around her little finger. He was infatuated with her and he'd do almost anything she suggested. She hoped she hadn't suggested too much.

"Which way will we go?" Bessie whispered as they mounted.

"Down the valley," Krause said. "The outlaws are up the valley by the wagons. We have to avoid them."

Bessie couldn't agree more. Avoiding them was the whole purpose of the mission. They walked their horses very slowly along the creek, well away from the camp. Once they got down the valley a way, Bessie began to relax.

"What will Sergeant Dodson say when he finds you missing?" she asked.

Krause laughed. "He'll know he's given me his last order. I've been thinking about deserting for some time. This is just the right time. With all that gold, we can really have a time."

"We're taking this gold to the bank in Omaha to help pay off the mortgage," Bessie said, feeling a surge of alarm.

"Why?" Krause asked. "You have only a small

part of it. That isn't going to do any good. That greedy banker is going to demand all of it or nothing."

A feeling of fear washed over Bessie. Pud Krause intended to spend this gold, not help her protect it. He was right that this small amount would never satisfy Atley Robinson. All Bessie had accomplished was to divide the gold. Neither she nor Stella had enough now to pay off the mortgage. Here she was less than a mile from camp and already she was seeing what a terrible mistake she had made.

"We'd better go back," she said softly.

"Go back?" Krause exclaimed. "Are you crazy? I've deserted. Do you know what they do with deserters? Shoot them, that's what. I'm not going back. And neither are you. Can't you guess what your sister will do to you when she finds out you stole some of her gold?"

"It's my gold, too," Bessie snapped. But her heart wasn't in the argument.

An hour ago that argument had seemed reason enough to do almost anything to get her hands on this gold. Now it had a hollow sound like the boom of a big drum.

Stella was all business, always had been. Her father had trusted Stella and her decisions on about everything. He never asked Bessie her opinion. Bessie had been sure that if Robinson could prevent them from paying off the mortgage so he could take over their mine and ranch, then Stella would have invested all of their gold in something. Bessie wanted a little of it to spend. She figured she wouldn't get it if Stella had control of it.

But now that Pud Krause had his fingers in the pie, she wondered if she'd get to spend any of this gold on herself. Krause was acting like a different man than he had at camp when he was bending over backward to help her in everything.

"When we get out of this valley, we'll go west," Krause said. "They will never expect us to go that way. We'll throw them off the trail quickly. Then we'll have a good time."

"We're going to Omaha with this gold," Bessie said, pushing herself to sound as confident as she thought Stella always did.

"Hold on now," Krause said. "You know that little dab you've got would just be wasted on that banker. He'd take it, all right, but he wouldn't tear up the mortgage. Why give the money to him? Let's enjoy it ourselves."

Bessie didn't say any more, but she began to consider wheeling her horse and galloping back to the camp. No matter what Stella did, it wouldn't be any worse than letting Krause spend all this gold.

Bessie couldn't see much in the dark, but she was guessing they were nearing the spot where the valley leveled out into the broader valley of the Platte. Here was where Krause intended to turn upstream and she was determined to go downstream toward Fort McPherson.

She was deep in thought when a rider suddenly appeared out of the darkness ahead of them. Even in the dimness, she could see the glint of the starlight on the gun barrel.

"Where are you heading?" he demanded.

"None of your business," Krause said sharply. "Just get out of our way."

"Getting away with some of the gold, I'll bet," the man said. "Hand it over."

Krause nudged his horse in front of Bessie. "You're not getting anything," he snapped.

"Just let me make sure you haven't got any gold," the gunman said. "Then I might let you go."

"You're not searching us, either," Krause said.

The private started to bring his rifle around. The man fired and Krause collapsed in the saddle and slid off to the ground. Bessie choked back a scream and jerked the reins on her horse.

The horse wheeled, but the man was quicker. He caught the bridle of Bessie's horse and brought him to a halt.

"Now let's see if you have the gold. Then I'll take you back to the boss. You have to be one of the Gordon girls."

He found the pouch of gold in a few seconds. Leaving the soldier where he had fallen, he took his horse, then tied Bessie's wrists to the horn of her saddle and led her horse, too.

When they headed up the valley, she was sure that this man belonged to Widlow's gang. They swung across the creek in a wide arc around the camp where the soldiers were. They passed the broken wagons and then suddenly were challenged by a sentry.

"Tell me who you are or you're dead."

"Nick Medder," the man said.

"I see two," came the retort.

"I have a prisoner. One of the Gordon girls."

"Come on," the sentry said. "Easy will be glad to see her."

Bessie was led past the sentry into a cove in the side of the valley. In a little niche that couldn't be seen from the main valley was a small fire. Three men were squatting around the tiny blaze. Bessie recognized one: Ken Sanford.

"Got something for you, Easy," Bessie's captor said.

A tall man got up from the fire and came forward. Bessie knew she was looking at the gang leader, Easy Widlow. She'd never heard of him till she came out with her father and sister to find the gold. She'd heard plenty about him since then.

Easy Widlow was a big man. Bessie guessed he must weigh over two hundred pounds. He wasn't a bad-looking man, and his eyes glowed like a cat's.

"Who are you?" he demanded.

She couldn't think of any lie with those eyes boring into her. "Bessie Gordon," she whispered.

Widlow switched his gaze to Nick Medder. "Did she have any of the gold with her?"

"Yep," Medder said and tossed the pouch to Widlow.

"Looks like we got lucky," Widlow said.

The two men remaining at the fire got up and came over. Sanford looked small compared to the second man, the biggest one of all. He was clearly Jud Bumbry, from the way Lane had described him.

"Now we've got the gold, we can go," Jud Bumbry said.

"That ain't all of it," Sanford said. "I put four bags like that in that axle."

"If there's more, we'll get it," Widlow said. He pointed at Medder. "Bring me that paper and pencil in my saddlebag."

Bessie watched her kidnapper move over to a saddle and rummage around inside the bag until he found a paper and a pencil. He brought them to Widlow.

Bessie studied the men around the fire. Four of them. Nick Medder had shot Pud Krause and kidnapped her. She knew Ken Sanford and now she could identify Jud Bumbry and Easy Widlow. There was a small man standing guard that she didn't know.

Now that Pud Krause was dead, there were only three soldiers and Lane Perry in the camp with Stella. The odds were in favor of the outlaws, especially since they were holding her as a hostage. There was no doubt in her mind what Widlow wanted the pencil and paper for.

The outlaw leader worked laboriously on the paper for a long time. Bessie watched him, realizing he barely knew how to write. When he had finished, he held out the paper for Bumbry to read.

"What does it say?" Sanford demanded.

"It ain't easy to read," Bumbry said. "But I reckon they'll figure it out. It says, 'We've got Bessie. If you want her back alive, bring the rest of the gold to the place where you find this note.' "

"Didn't you sign it?" Sanford asked.

"Sure, I signed it," Widlow said. "I want them to know I mean business."

"How are you going to get this to them?" Sanford asked.

"I suggest we send Sanford," Bumbry suggested. "He can ride right into their camp with it."

"Oh, no," Sanford snorted. "You can just figure another way."

"I've got it figured," Widlow said, scowling at the two men. "You can stop your sparring. We may have trouble and we don't need any fighting among us." He looked at Medder. "Take this down close to their camp. Find a spot where they can't miss it. Put this paper there. Then fire your gun. They'll come to investigate and find the note. You hide somewhere and see what they do. I figure they'll bring the gold out there pronto."

"What about Turley?" Medder asked. "We didn't find him where he went down."

"He dropped like a dead weight," Widlow said. "He was killed."

"Then how did he get away from the place where he fell?"

"Those soldiers probably found him and buried him with all the others," Widlow said. "It's no skin off our noses."

"What if he's still alive and a prisoner of the soldiers?"

"If he is, he'd better keep his mouth shut," Widlow said. "We ain't going to worry about Fel. We're going to concentrate on getting that gold and getting out of the country. Get going, Nick."

Medder went to his horse and mounted. Bessie watched him go. With her hands tied and the outlaws close by, there wasn't much else she could do. If she could escape and get back to the soldiers' camp, she could save the gold Stella still had. But even if she could get free, the chances were that Stella would make her decision about the rest of the gold before she could get back there. She had made a big mess of everything.

Bessie's attention was taken from her own troubles by raised voices over by the fire. She saw that it was Sanford and Bumbry arguing again. Apparently they didn't get along well.

"I want to know why everybody was killed in the wagons," Sanford said.

"Jud didn't want any survivors to tell what had happened," Widlow said, shrugging as if it were an unimportant thing.

"Four men died there, and there was nothing gained by it," Sanford said. "Everybody knows who did it, anyway."

"They wouldn't have if we'd got Lane Perry," Bumbry snapped.

"Why didn't you get him?"

"He was out hunting," Widlow said. "We didn't know about him, and Jud forgot about him till it was too late to trap him."

"You were a poor one to put in charge of the wagons," Sanford said disgustedly to Bumbry.

Bumbry scowled at the mine foreman. "Why didn't you just steal the gold when you were putting it in the wagons? That would have been simpler."

"I couldn't do that. They'd have known it was me," Sanford snapped. "Let's divide what gold we have now."

"You'd want the hog's share," Bumbry growled.

"I want my third of it," Sanford said. "That's what I was to get for giving you the information.

Remember, you'd never have had any idea that gold was in your wagons if I hadn't told you."

"That's another thing," Bumbry roared. "You didn't tell us where it was. If we'd have known, we could have gotten it and been gone long before this."

"If you'd known where it was, you'd have stolen it yourself and none of the rest of us would have gotten a pinch of it," Sanford yelled back.

"Calm down, you two!" Widlow snapped. "Stop fighting! We know where the gold is now and we're going to get it."

"And I get my third," Sanford said.

"You greedy hog!" Bumbry roared. "You didn't turn a finger except to tell us the gold was in those wagons. I did all the work of leading the wagons and bringing them into this valley where Easy could get to them without running into other travelers. I should get half for what I did."

"Hold on now," Widlow put in calmly. "I was offered half for getting it away from Gordon. The way you've divided it, I wouldn't get much. Now you know me better than that. I'm going to get my half, at least."

The two men scowled at Widlow, but neither argued the point. Bessie saw the power that Easy Widlow had over the other men. But it didn't stop the argument between Bumbry and Sanford. Each wanted a major share of the half that Widlow wouldn't take.

The sun had been up a couple of hours now, but nobody made any move to do anything but wait for Medder to return. They had heard his revolver shot some time ago and all knew that it was up to Stella Gordon now whether they got the gold handed to them or whether they would have to fight for it.

Bumbry told Sanford that he was going to take the half that Widlow didn't get, and Sanford could like it or not. He stamped away and Sanford followed him, arguing at the top of his voice. They went around a bulge in the valley wall out of sight of the camp.

Only when two shots rang out back there did Easy Widlow jerk up his head. Apparently he had thought that his orders not to quarrel were enough to stop any serious trouble. Widlow strode out toward the spot where the shots had sounded. He met Jud Bumbry coming toward camp.

Bessie watched as Bumbry and Widlow came back to the spot where the ashes of the fire still smoldered.

"You didn't need to kill him," Widlow snapped angrily.

"He drew on me," Bumbry said. "Anyway, he didn't earn a share of the gold."

"Let's get one thing settled," Widlow said. "I'll decide who gets what share. Understand?"

Widlow's pale eyes bored into Bumbry. Bumbry was bigger than Widlow and he returned the glare, but slowly his eyes dropped and he nodded as he shuffled off to his bedroll to sit and wait for Medder's return. Bessie realized why Easy Widlow was the leader. Nobody overruled him.

Widlow called the guard back from his sentry duties. "Let's get things gathered up, Copo. We're going to move farther into the canyons south of here."

"What about the Gordon girl?" Bumbry asked after a time. "Do we let her go if they give us the gold?"

"We'll think about that," Widlow said.

A chill ran over Bessie. She couldn't be sure she wouldn't be killed even if Stella turned over the rest of the gold. And she wasn't at all sure that Stella would do that. Her older sister was stubborn; she might think there was a way to get Bessie back without giving up the gold. The way Bessie saw it, there wasn't. And she wasn't even sure she'd get back alive if Stella did turn over the other pouches.

Medder rode into the camp before noon, announcing that they had come out to investigate his shot and found the note on a rock where he'd left it, anchored by a small stone.

"Did they act like they would bring the gold?" Widlow asked.

Medder shook his head. "They didn't fall over themselves getting back to their camp to get the gold. I waited for two hours. They never came back."

"We head for the canyons south of here," Widlow announced.

"We'll never get the gold that way," Bumbry shouted.

"We'll get it," Widlow said. "That girl over there isn't going to leave her sister in my hands. They'll follow us into the canyons. We can trap them in the canyons and get the gold."

Bessie had a deep feeling that Stella was not going to give up that gold to gain her freedom. She'd been frightened ever since Medder had captured her, but now that fear gripped her like paralysis.

VII

Lane wasn't sure what to do. He had no idea how long Bessie and Krause had been gone. There was little doubt in his mind that they had run off together with the one pouch of gold that was missing. It hurt him to think that Bessie would run off with another man. But then he remembered she had practically offered him the same opportunity that Krause had apparently accepted.

Bessie was determined to have some of that gold. Or else she was afraid they'd never get it to the Omaha bank as long as Widlow's gang was shadowing the soldier escort. Maybe she thought she could slip it through without the gang finding out.

If that was the case, why didn't she take it all? It didn't make sense to take part of the gold and not all if she was trying to slip it past Widlow to the train and on to Omaha. Just part of the payment would never satisfy a banker like Atley Robinson.

"We'd better get on the trail if we expect to overtake them," Lane said. "No telling how far ahead of us they are."

"I should have kept an eye on Bessie," Stella said. "I just didn't think she'd do such a thing."

"Maybe she hasn't," Lane said softly. "Maybe we're jumping to conclusions."

"I'd rather jump to that conclusion than to think what else might have happened to her," Stella said.

The sergeant got his horse saddled and assigned Private Lyon to get his and Private Voage's horses ready and to take the prisoner, Turley, with him. Voage was still on guard duty. Lane got his own horse and Stella's ready.

"Bessie's horse is gone," he told Stella when he brought her horse. "So is Krause's. Looks like they rode off on their own accord."

"We must find them quickly," Stella said. "If we don't, that soldier may have all the gold spent."

Lane knew that was a good bet. Stella got the other pouches of gold. With the horses saddled, they mounted and started moving. They hadn't cleaned up the camp, but speed was more important now.

They had gone no more than a quarter of a mile when a shot up the valley brought them to an abrupt halt.

"Who would be shooting back there?" Dodson demanded. "Maybe we're guessing wrong. Maybe they went that way and ran into Widlow's gang."

"Sounded close to our camp," Voage said.

"Come on, Lane," Dodson said. "We'll investigate. The rest of you wait here or come back to camp."

Lane fell in beside the sergeant and the others trailed behind.

"Easy does it," the sergeant said as they passed the camp. "It may be an ambush."

Lane had already considered that possibility. He had also thought of the chance that it might be a message from Bessie. He didn't trust Bessie's judgment to keep her out of trouble. And he hadn't been overly impressed with Private Krause.

Lane reined up a couple of hundred yards beyond their old camp. "I estimate that shot came from about this far away," he said.

Dodson nodded. "I agree. Let's leave our horses and advance on foot."

Dodson carried his rifle at the ready while Lane had his revolver in his hand as they moved forward.

Lane saw the rock first. There weren't many rocks around, so this one stood out on the grassy slope. And something on it was fluttering in the morning breeze.

"Cover me," Lane said. "I'll see what it is."

He moved up to the rock, searching the area around. There was a gully running back from the valley less than fifty yards away, but he tried to ignore it. If anyone was watching, that would be where he would be. If he charged out of there, Lane would be ready.

Reaching the rock, his eyes fell on the paper, held in place by the stone, with the crude printing on it. He had no trouble making out what it said. He picked up the note and retreated to the sergeant.

"The gang has Bessie," he said, handing the paper to Dodson. "The note is signed by Easy Widlow."

"Easy Widlow has been robbing travelers along the trail for some time," Dodson said. "He never tackles a big train. I figure he has a small gang. Doesn't rouse so much public demand for action, either, like he would if he held up a big train." He looked at the note. "How did he know there was more gold?"

"Same way he knew there was any gold at all in those wagons," Lane said. "Stella thinks Ken Sanford might have gone over to Widlow's gang. Sanford was the one who put that gold in the axle."

"It's a shame to lose that gold after going to all this trouble getting it this close to Omaha," Dodson said.

"Will Widlow release Bessie even if Stella gives him the money?"

Dodson frowned. "I don't know. Widlow leads a charmed life. Everybody who knows him says he's invincible. I've never seen a man who couldn't be whipped by someone. But then I've never seen Easy Widlow."

"You think he's capable of killing Bessie even if he gets the money?"

Dodson spread his hands. "All I know is what I've heard about him. And that isn't good."

"I suppose we'll have to turn over the gold on the chance that he'll release her," Lane said. "Let's go back and show this to Stella."

Lane wasn't sure what Stella's reaction would be to the note. She was a stubborn person. Turning the gold over to Widlow would not be her way of doing things.

She looked at the paper and studied it as a teacher might study a pupil's lesson.

"Do we take the rest of the gold out to Widlow?" Lane asked.

"Not unless there is absolutely no other way," Stella said.

"What other way do you suggest?" Lane asked.

"I don't know until I think about it. Where is Widlow's camp?"

"I'll have to find out," Lane said. "Some of Widlow's men may be watching to see what we're going to do. So make it look like we're trying to make a decision. I'll try to find his camp and see what kind of a situation we're facing."

For over an hour, they huddled together as though discussing possibilities. Then Lane got his horse. There was no way he could hide his movements in the open valley, even if he stayed in the willows. A horse thrashing through the little trees would attract as much attention as a bull moose wading in a river.

Moving up the valley, Lane found the spot where the outlaws had camped. But there was no one there now. The place looked as if it had just been abandoned.

Lane rode cautiously up the valley and hadn't gone far before he turned a slight corner and saw the caravan ahead of him. He recognized the huge bulk of Jud Bumbry. There were three other men. One of them would be Easy Widlow, but he couldn't see which one.

They were riding in a sort of box formation with Bessie right in the middle of the box. Maybe they anticipated someone trailing them and they were making it virtually impossible for anyone to take a shot at them without risking an injury to Bessie. Lane actually considered trying a shot at Jud Bumbry. But it was a long shot, and there was the distinct possibility of hitting Bessie. Even if he hit his man, Bessie would be thrown into immediate danger from the others.

He watched them for a while. They were definitely moving south. That was canyon country over there in the watershed of the Republican River. Obviously they were sure that the soldiers would not take the gold on to the fort until they had rescued Bessie.

Lane reined around and headed back to camp. If they were going to follow the gang and try to rescue Bessie, they'd have to start soon or they would lose their trail. There was no question in Lane's mind that they had to follow Widlow, although he felt sure that Widlow was expecting that and likely had moved just to get them to break camp and follow. An ambush somewhere in the canyons ahead would be a logical reason for this move.

Putting his horse to a lope, Lane covered the ground quickly. He passed Private Voage standing guard above the camp and motioned him to come into the circle of the camp. Sergeant Dodson, Private Lyon, and Stella were waiting for Lane.

"What did you find?" Dodson demanded.

"They're pulling out. Heading toward the canyon country south of here."

"Did you see Bessie?" Stella demanded.

"She was with them," Lane said.

"Can we get her away from them?" Stella asked next.

"Not without a fight, I'm afraid," Lane said. "They were riding in a bunch and had her right in the middle. I couldn't risk a shot at any of them for fear of hitting her."

"Was Private Krause with them?" Dodson asked.

"I didn't see him," Lane said.

"Then they must have killed him," Dodson said. "They couldn't expect any ransom for him. We'll have to find his body."

"What about Bessie?" Lane asked.

Dodson bit his lip. "My first duty is to my men," he said.

"What about the people you were escorting out here?" Lane demanded.

Dodson frowned, then nodded. "They're my responsibility, too. I wish I knew what happened to Krause."

"We can both guess," Lane said. "But we know what has happened to Bessie. Isn't it your duty to help the living?"

"If I was to handle all my duties right now, I'd need a company of men, not just a two-man squad."

"I'm going after Bessie," Stella said flatly.

Dodson looked at the determination in Stella's face, then back at Lane. "I can do only one of the jobs I'm supposed to do. I don't go along with kidnapping. We'll go after Bessie and just hope I'm not neglecting my duty to Private Krause. Get your horses," he yelled at the two remaining privates.

"I'll ride ahead and scout," Lane volunteered.

"I'll appreciate that. But take care. That is canyon country down south. I've been there on patrol. Unlimited opportunities for ambushes."

"What about our prisoner?" Lyon asked.

Dodson rubbed his chin. "He has to go in for trial."

"You might do what those thieves have

probably done to Krause," Voage suggested.

"I want to see him shot legally," Dodson said.

"What will we do with him now?" Lane asked. "He's going to be a liability while we're trying to follow Widlow's gang."

"Reckon he will," Dodson agreed. "Private Voage, you'll take responsibility for bringing the prisoner along with us."

Voage frowned, but he nodded. "All right."

Lane heard Voage give a warning to the outlaw.

"I hope you'll try to escape. I'd rather shoot you than lug you all the way back to the fort."

Turley didn't say anything. Lane watched Voage lash Turley to his saddle.

Turley started to roar. "I told you everything I knew about Easy Widlow and his gang. That ought to be worth something to you."

"It is," Voage said. "It may keep us all from getting ambushed."

"It ought to be enough to make you turn me loose," Turley said. "If I'd known you were going to kill me, anyway, I wouldn't have told you nothing."

"My orders are not to kill you," Voage said. "They're to keep you alive. But I can't see why. Your buddies evidently killed one of my buddies."

Turley scowled, but he refused to say anymore. Lane rode out in front as the caravan began moving up the valley. Staying in sight of the others, he pointed the way that he had seen

Widlow's outfit go. Then he nudged his horse into a lope to gain on the kidnappers.

He came in sight of the outlaws sooner than he expected. They had stopped, apparently resting. Lane reined over to a spot where he was hidden and watched. The outlaws had dismounted and were looking back, as if they expected to be followed.

Lane checked the men twice before he was certain that there were only three. There had been four when he'd seen them earlier. He couldn't tell which one was missing, but he could think of only one reason why one was gone. He might be coming back to pick off some of the followers. Or perhaps they knew now that Fel Turley was a prisoner of the army and they wanted to get him free.

Lane stayed out of sight and watched a minute longer. The outlaws were casting frequent glances back toward the valley where they had been. Lane didn't find it so hard to hide here because they were at the edge of the deep canyon country.

It was evident that the outlaws were not going to move on right away. They were waiting for something, likely for the return of the man who was missing from the group. Since they kept casting glances over their back trail, Lane guessed the missing man had come this way. Lane decided he had to find him before the gunman got close to Sergeant Dodson's group.

Reining back, he kept out of sight of the outlaws ahead and backtracked his own trail. Then he saw the missing gunman. The man was back in a gully almost directly in front of Lane. And he was concentrating on Dodson's advancing group. Lane wondered what the man intended to do, but whatever it was, it could cause someone to be shot.

Reining to his left, Lane moved in close to the man, who still hadn't taken his eyes off the soldiers. Dismounting, Lane moved ahead on foot. He was too close to Widlow's men to be out of their hearing. If he fired a gun, it could bring on a fight. With Stella in this group and Bessie in the other, a gun battle was the last thing Lane wanted.

Lane guessed the gunman was either spying on the soldiers or planning to rescue Turley. Private Voage was well behind the rest of the group with Turley. It might be possible to slip up behind Voage and grab Turley. Whatever the man was intending to do, he was totally concentrating on his plans.

Rocks had fallen from the low bluff rimming the little gully where the man was waiting. Lane carefully picked his way through the small rocks, but his foot hit one when he was only a few feet from the man. The rock threw him off balance and, in catching himself, he made enough noise to jerk the man's attention from the soldiers to himself.

The man wheeled and Lane lunged at him. He had to keep the man from using his gun and he didn't want to do any shooting himself. The man jumped to meet Lane. He made no move for his gun, either. Likely he was just as eager to avoid shooting because he was very close to the soldiers.

Even though the gunman was surprised, he was ready for battle. He was quite strong—thirty pounds heavier than Lane but not as tall. Lane used his extra reach to sting him and dodge away. He didn't intend to get close enough that the man could use his strength to overpower him.

It was obvious from the first move that the other man was a brawler. Lane kept out of his way and slapped him hard with his fists. Then he saw an opening and put all his strength behind a blow to his chin. It snapped the man's head back and he went down. But he scrambled up quickly.

Boring in, swinging wildly, the man came at Lane. Lane dodged, but one blow caught him on the side of the head. An explosion of light flashed in front of his eyes.

Before Lane blacked out, he was conscious of the fact that the man had a rock gripped in his fist and it was that rock that had hit him.

When Lane revived, he had no idea how long he had been out. The man he had been fighting was gone. So was the man's horse. He steadied himself as he sat up and looked around. He saw that Dodson had brought his group to a stop and camped not far from where they had been when Lane had attacked Widlow's man. He also noticed that it was getting dark. He must have been out for some time.

His head felt as if someone were using an ax to split it. He was surprised that he was still alive. The man apparently didn't wait around long enough to kill him. He wondered why Dodson had camped here. He hadn't moved much since Lane saw him last, and there had been plenty of time to move on.

It was not long before Lane got himself in shape to ride out to the camp. Dodson met him, demanding an explanation. Lane gave it to him as best he could. Then he asked about camping here. Dodson explained that they had discovered Widlow camping a short distance ahead and decided it was best to wait until he got Lane's report before attempting a rescue of Bessie.

Lane started in search of Stella to get her opinion of the situation. He was sure she would have an idea how to attempt a rescue. He couldn't find her. In a small camp like this, that seemed ridiculous.

Then it hit him. Stella was gone. He could think of only one reason. She had decided to rescue Bessie herself. A chill ran over him. She could never pull it off against Easy Widlow.

VIII

Stella had waited impatiently for Lane Perry to return from his scouting mission. She could see no reason why he hadn't come back. Private Lyon had ridden ahead to see if he could locate Lane. He had come back to report that Widlow's camp was just ahead. It appeared they planned to spend the night there. He had gotten close enough to make sure that Lane Perry was not a prisoner there. So where was he?

Stella tried to think what she should do now. Worry plagued her thoughts. Having Bessie a prisoner of an outlaw like Easy Widlow was worry enough, but now Lane was missing, too. Not that Lane was anything special. It was just that she had depended so much on him. He gave her a feeling that whatever he set out to do, he'd accomplish. Now the thought nagged at her that something bad had happened to him.

She just couldn't take any more. She had never been one to sit back and wait for things to come to her. She was a firm believer that good things came to those who went after them. She wanted Bessie out of the grasp of the outlaws. If Lane hadn't figured a way to do it, then she'd have to do it herself.

That responsibility didn't bother her. But how

was she to accomplish the feat? When it began to get dark, Stella decided that Lane was not coming back. She had waited long enough. Something had to be done and it was up to her to do it.

Then she thought of the gold she had been guarding. She could not take that with her on a mission to the enemy camp. The one thing she certainly did not intend to do was let those outlaws get their hands on it. Where could she hide it so no one could find it?

She considered half a dozen places and turned thumbs down on them almost as quickly as they came to mind. Then she thought of the soldier who was so particular with his gear. Private Oliver Voage kept everything in perfect order even when they were moving from one spot to another.

Voage's gear was in a neat pile at the edge of camp now, while he was standing guard over the prisoner, Turley. If she could slip her gold into his gear somewhere, it would be safe. She wouldn't dare tell him about it. She wouldn't tell anyone.

Taking the pouches and concealing them under a light jacket she had brought, Stella moved over close to Voage's things. She spotted the soldier's raincoat neatly folded at the bottom of his pack where it had been since they had left Fort McPherson. It didn't look like rain now, either. He wasn't likely to unfold that raincoat until they got back to Fort McPherson.

If she could get those pouches of gold into that raincoat, nobody would find them. No thief would think to look in a soldier's gear for them.

Making sure no one was watching, Stella stooped and opened the folds of the raincoat and slipped the pouches inside. Then she folded the coat back so the gold couldn't slip out. She'd get the pouches back as soon as she returned from her mission.

With that done, she turned her attention to getting away from camp. Sergeant Dodson was talking to his two privates, Voage and Lyon, assigning them guard posts. Turley would not need a special guard while they were camped. Dodson would relieve one guard later. If Lane came back, he could relieve the other guard. They began a serious discussion as to what might have befallen Lane. Stella took advantage of their concentration to slip out of camp.

In the deepening shadows, she began the descent into the canyons where the outlaws had their camp, according to Lyon's scouting report. She didn't think she would have any trouble finding the camp. She was sure the outlaws wanted them to find it. Maybe they would really trade Bessie for the rest of the gold.

Stella wasn't at all sure that they would live up to their end of that bargain, though. If she thought they would, she would probably turn over the gold. It went against everything she stood for to give up that mine and ranch when they had those riches right in their hands, but the life of her sister was worth more than the mine.

However, Stella didn't trust outlaws like Easy Widlow. Once he got the gold, there was no telling what he would do to Bessie. There had to be a better way of freeing her.

As she moved along, she tried to think of some way of diverting the attention of the men in the enemy camp while she freed Bessie. Maybe her best chance would be to try to slip in during the night unnoticed and get Bessie away. In thinking about it, she was sure she would have a better chance alone than with the sergeant and his soldiers along. Force was about all the army understood, she was sure. If they started a battle, even if they won it, Bessie would likely be killed before it was over. Stella wondered how far away the enemy camp would be. If she could get close enough to attract Bessie's attention, she would work out something.

She thought back to the games they had played when they were girls. Bessie was three years younger than Stella. They used to have a secret whistle that sounded much like a bird with which they called the other's attention without alerting their parents that they were communicating. That whistle might work again. But that would depend on the situation when she found the camp.

Stella almost stumbled into the camp. She

hadn't expected it quite so close. Darkness had filled the canyons, and this little canyon seemed particularly dark. But now that she was aware of the camp, she could make out some features of it. She knelt in the grass and studied it.

There were four men in a small area and when a spark suddenly blazed up, she saw that they were building a small fire. Evidently they didn't care who knew they were here. In fact, it almost appeared as if they wanted to be found.

Look as hard as she would, Stella couldn't locate Bessie. When the fire was going, a small man broke away from the group and moved off into the darkness at the edge of the firelight. Stella followed him with her eyes. It was then that she saw her sister. There was a rock against the canyon wall and Bessie was backed up against that, sitting on the grass. From the way she was sitting, Stella knew her hands were tied and maybe her feet were, too.

The guard—the small man—squatted down against another rock not too far away. Stella stole closer. She had to get to Bessie without the guard seeing her or Bessie might be dead. Stella would probably be, too. That would solve everything for Atley Robinson. Hank Gordon was dead. If both his daughters were dead, too, there would be nobody to contest the banker's taking over the ranch and the mine.

Stella studied the situation. The guard was on

the other side of Bessie. If she could alert Bessie that she was there so Bessie wouldn't make a sound, she might slip over and untie her without the guard noticing. Then maybe Bessie could slowly inch around the rock and the two of them could disappear into the night.

The scheme looked possible to Stella. It was dangerous. She knew that. But she couldn't see any alternative. She must not fail. Failing frightened her more than the danger involved.

Softly Stella gave the whistle that the two girls had used when they were youngsters. The first whistle didn't seem to reach Bessie. Stella checked the guard. He hadn't moved or even looked her way.

She whistled again, a bit louder than before. Bessie lifted her head and slowly turned to look Stella's way. Stella didn't move, but she knew that Bessie had heard. Now she had to move silently over to Bessie and untie her.

Ever so slowly, she moved forward, crouching so low that she didn't think the guard on the far side of the rock could see her. A few more feet and she would be close enough to reach Bessie.

Bessie had turned her head toward Stella now and her eyes were wide. Stella guessed this was the first real hope of escape she'd had since she had been captured. Bessie lifted her bound hands as if to stifle a scream. Stella frowned. Movement like that could attract the attention of the guard.

"Going somewhere, lady?" a voice said directly behind Stella.

Bessie screamed and Stella almost did. She thought screaming was a sign of weakness and she had never considered herself weak. But right now her knees were so weak she was sure they wouldn't hold her up. Her head seemed about to burst, and she thought she couldn't get her breath. Was she going to faint?

Spinning around, she stared at the heavyset man. He was holding a gun in his hand. Stella knew she had no chance against him. He looked strong enough to wrestle a bull.

The small man who had been guarding Bessie came rushing over from the spot where he'd been sitting.

"What have you got, Nick?" he demanded.

"I caught what you should have caught, Dorse," Nick Medder said. "You were supposed to watch the prisoner."

"I was," the little man said. "I didn't see anything."

"That's what I mean. You're supposed to see everything. In a couple more minutes this lady would have had your prisoner free and they'd have been gone. Think how Easy would have liked that."

The other two men came over from the fire.

"Copo, what's going on?" Widlow demanded.

The little man, Dorse Copo, stuttered that Nick had caught a girl sneaking into camp.

Widlow wheeled to the heavyset man. "What about that, Medder?"

"She was fixing to spring your prisoner," Nick said.

"Who is she?"

"Haven't had time to ask any questions yet," Medder said.

"I'll find out who she is," Dorse Copo said, trying to redeem himself in the eyes of Widlow.

"I'll do it," Nick Medder said. "I caught her."

"Shut up, both of you," Widlow snapped. He looked at Jud Bumbry. "Know her?"

"Sure," Bumbry said. "That's the other Gordon girl. Now we've got both of them. Not much question now whether we get the gold or not."

Widlow nodded. He motioned to Medder. "Tie her up beside the other one while we decide on the next move. And make sure she can't get away."

Medder was none too gentle as he bound Stella's wrists together, then tied another rope around her ankles. Then he helped her to a sitting position beside Bessie.

"Now, Dorse, keep a sharp eye on them," Nick said. "If you let them get away, you'd better shoot yourself. That won't be as messy as what Easy will do to you."

"They won't get away," Copo said. He moved

around where he had a good view of both girls and the surrounding area.

"I tried to warn you about Medder," Bessie said softly when all but Copo were gone.

"I guess I was too intent on getting you loose without that guard seeing me," Stella said. "I didn't think about there being two guards."

"There wasn't," Bessie said. "I think Medder just happened to see you. Copo has been guarding me most of the time."

Stella was trying to organize her thinking. She wasn't in the habit of having her plans completely overturned like this. She had recognized the possibility of failure and had made decisions regarding her next move. But she had made no allowance for her capture. Now she had to begin all over and from a most disadvantageous position.

"You've been a captive for quite a while," Stella said. "What kind of an escape plan have you worked out?"

"There's no way we can escape from them," Bessie said. "They keep a close watch on me so I gave up thinking about escaping."

Stella scowled. "You never give up!" she snapped. "That's only for suckers. We're going to get out of this. I don't know how yet, but we will."

Bessie seemed to brighten. She had always followed Stella's lead when things got bad.

"Maybe they will let us go when they get the gold," Bessie said hopefully.

"We're not going to let them have that gold," Stella snapped.

"How are you going to stop them? When they tell Lane and the sergeant that we're both prisoners, they'll make the decision about the ransom."

"They won't find the gold," Stella said.

It struck her that if it should actually come down to their lives or the gold, it could cost them their lives because she doubted that anybody in the soldiers' camp could find the gold, unless Private Voage should accidentally find it.

After a long conference, Widlow and Bumbry came back to Stella and Bessie.

"Our offer still goes," Widlow said smugly. "That gold for your lives. It's as simple as that."

"We'll do it," Bessie said quickly.

"You've been saying that," Widlow said, "but what you say here doesn't carry much weight with the soldiers over there. Now I figure that it will be different since we have both of you."

"Why do you think that will make a difference?" Stella demanded.

"From what Jud tells me he's heard, you are the kingpin in the Gordon family. There'll be nobody over there now to balk at turning over the gold."

Stella drew in her breath to tell them that nobody over there knew where the gold was, then decided against it. Let them make the offer to Sergeant Dodson. It would take time for the soldiers and Lane to look for the gold. Stella was betting they wouldn't find it. The time that would buy would be time she and Bessie could use trying to figure a way to escape.

She turned her anger on Bumbry. "You're the double-crossing turncoat that caused my father's death," she snapped. "You won't live to enjoy any gain."

Bumbry chuckled. "Now ain't you the one to tell me what I can do?"

"You're not going to get any gold," Stella snapped. "Not even if you kill us!"

Bumbry stopped laughing, his brow pulling down into a frown. "Oh, I'll get half of that gold, all right."

Widlow shook his head at Bumbry. "Easy, friend," he said softly. "Just because you got rid of Sanford doesn't mean your share is going to be any bigger than it was."

"I suppose you're going to take Sanford's share," Bumbry growled.

"You're supposing just right," Widlow said. "But we have to get the gold before we can divide it."

Bumbry's face was livid, but he made no move to argue the point. Maybe it was the presence of Nick Medder, just behind Widlow, and Dorse Copo, guarding the girls but ready to take a hand in case of trouble, that stopped him.

"As long as you hold the girls, you've accomplished what you were told to do," Bumbry said.

"That's right," Widlow said. "But the payoff as far as you and me are concerned is that gold. Now let's put our heads together and get that. Then if we have to fight over how it's divided, there will be plenty of opportunity for that."

Stella could see that Bumbry was whipped. He was bigger than Widlow, but he wasn't as strong-willed. Sergeant Dodson had said he'd heard that people called Widlow invincible. She was beginning to see what he meant.

Widlow laboriously wrote another note, saying he had both girls and they'd be killed if the gold wasn't forfeited immediately. He let Stella and Bessie see the note before he sent it back to the soldiers' camp.

"Now, little lady," he said to Stella, "you'd better send word to your soldier friends where that gold is in case you hid it so they can find it to bring to me."

Bessie begged Stella to comply, almost in hysteria. Stella was finding it hard to keep her resolve, but she was certain their lives weren't any more in danger if Widlow didn't get the gold than if he did.

She shook her head. "Let the soldiers find the gold themselves," she said sharply.

"I never saw anybody as anxious to die as you

are," Widlow snapped. He handed the note to Medder. "Take that close to their camp, fire your gun, then get back here."

Stella gritted her teeth. Maybe Bessie was right. Maybe she should tell them where the gold was hidden. She doubted if she could buy enough time to think of a way for Bessie and her to escape. Her only hope, she knew, was Lane Perry. She had almost unlimited faith in him. But she would never let anyone know how she felt. She remembered that Lane had been long overdue back at camp when she had slipped out to come to Bessie's rescue. Likely something had happened to him. Even if he was all right, what could he do?

"We'll give them three hours to come up with the gold," Widlow said loud enough for Stella to hear. "If they don't, then we'll leave them two dead girls to bury."

Bessie wailed loudly, losing control of herself. Stella held a rigid face. She wouldn't give Widlow the satisfaction of knowing the despair she really felt. If Lane was back at the soldiers' camp, he would make some effort to save them. She was sure of that.

But then Widlow wiped out that faint hope. "Pack up," he told Copo and Bumbry. "We're moving further back into the canyons where they can't find us. We wanted them to find us so they'd bargain. That time is past. If they want to bargain, they'll have to make the next move."

"What about Nick?" Copo said. "If we move, he can't find us."

"You'll stay here and meet Nick when he comes back," Widlow said. "Jud will guard the girls till you get back to camp. We'll go to our hideout in Busby Canyon. You tell Nick to watch for them when they come to bring the gold and direct them to us. Let's get moving."

Stella realized they were going to be taken to Widlow's secret hideout. Even Lane wouldn't be able to find them there.

IX

Lane and Sergeant Dodson had discussed the probability that Stella had gone on a solo attempt to rescue her sister. Both agreed that such an extreme venture was well within Stella's capabilities. Both also agreed that she wouldn't have the chance of a mouse in a hawk's nest of succeeding.

Dodson wanted to wait to see if Stella returned. He was afraid that they would only increase the danger to her if they tried to overtake her and bring her back. Lane agreed to wait a while but not too long.

Every minute he waited, his anxiety grew. Lane hadn't felt this uneasy when Bessie disappeared. He had thought he was falling in love with Bessie, but maybe it was the fact that she had run off with Private Krause that had dampened his enthusiasm for her.

He certainly had no reason to be any more concerned about Stella than he had been about Bessie. But he was and he didn't understand why? She didn't fix herself up the way Bessie did. She dressed plainly, pulled her hair back into a plain knot on her head, and made no attempt to be attractive. And she was stubborn. She was right most of the time, he admitted, but she was adamant about her decisions. Yet in spite of all that, he couldn't help thinking he'd do almost anything to make sure Stella was safe right now.

The darkness seemed to close in on the head of the canyon where they were camped. It seemed darker to Lane when he thought of Stella out there somewhere probably making a foolhardy attempt to rescue her sister. If anybody was going to risk his life to save Bessie, it ought to be him.

"Let's go after her," Lane said finally. "If she was coming back, she should have been here by now."

Dodson nodded. "I'm afraid you're right. She's a brave girl, but bravery isn't enough when you're dealing with the likes of Easy Widlow."

"She seems like a reasonable girl," Lane said. "Why would she think she could rescue Bessie herself?"

"She's also a stubborn girl and quite capable," Dodson said. "I imagine Stella probably thought she could pull it off."

"I'm sure she did or she wouldn't have tried it—if that is what she has done."

Lane tried to find something positive in his own words. But just thinking she could do it and actually accomplishing it were two different things, especially when dealing with outlaws like Easy Widlow's gang.

"It looks like we're up against a tough situation," Dodson said. "I wish we had some reinforcements."

"An all-out battle would likely result in Widlow killing Bessie," Lane said.

Dodson chewed his lip. "Maybe. Widlow is a tough one. The army has bumped into him before and we've never come out on top."

Suddenly a shot echoed in the canyon just a short distance to the south. Lane and Dodson wheeled that way. Dodson jerked his head back toward the camp to make sure both Voage and Lyon were there. The sergeant hadn't posted a guard yet. Lane thought he might be figuring on moving farther down the canyon before camping for the night.

"Can't be a fight," Dodson said.

"Likely a message from Widlow," Lane said, dreading the implication of that.

Lane started down the canyon with Dodson at his heels. He moved cautiously. He wasn't discounting the possibility that Widlow would use this ruse to get him and Dodson away from the other soldiers to ambush them. They had responded to the first signal and the outlaws could be sure they would respond to this one, too.

Lane saw the paper on the rock, with the stone on top, but he didn't see anyone nearby. He stopped and tried to pierce the darkness beyond the rock but could see nothing. The paper was no more than a few yards away. If it was an ambush, the trap would be sprung when he reached for the note.

He took the chance and got the paper in his hand without a shot being fired. Dodson suggested in a whisper that they take the note back to camp before lighting a match to read it. Lane agreed.

At camp, Dodson struck a match and Lane read the note by its flickering light. He lowered the paper and looked at the sergeant.

"They've got Stella, too," he said tonelessly.

"They're demanding all the gold or we'll have two dead girls to bury."

"We've got no choice," Dodson said. "Let's get the gold."

"Stella might object even if she is the one to be ransomed."

"She isn't making the decisions now," Dodson said. "Let's get the gold."

"Widlow may murder both girls even if we do turn over the gold," Lane said.

"He might," Dodson agreed. "But then he might not. We know he will if he doesn't get the gold. So let's take a chance he'll do what he says and turn them loose once he gets the gold."

Dodson headed for the roll of belongings of Stella and Bessie Gordon. Lane doubted if this was what Stella would want. But he saw no other way unless they made an attempt to rescue the girls themselves. That would be very risky both to themselves and the girls.

Dodson returned after a couple of minutes. “There’s no gold in their baggage. She’s hidden it somewhere.”

“I suppose she knows where it is,” Lane said. “But that isn’t doing us any good now.”

The sergeant turned to the two privates. “Lyon,” he called. “Get your horse ready. I’m sending you back to Fort McPherson with a message. We have to have reinforcements. Widlow has captured both the Gordon girls and we need help in getting them back.”

“A pitched battle may get them killed,” Lane objected.

“Maybe Widlow will abandon them when he sees the force coming against him. He understands strength. Ten or fifteen soldiers will look overpowering to him.”

“How long will it take Lyon to get there?”

“If he rides hard, he can be there before morning,” Dodson said. He knelt and began writing by the dim light of the night sky. When he finished, Private Lyon was standing behind him with his horse.

“Give this to the colonel,” Dodson said, handing Lyon the note.

“What about Turley?” Voage asked. “We ought to get him to the fort. He’s a real liability to us now.”

“I realize that,” Dodson said. “But I can’t slow Lyon down with a prisoner. We’ll just have to hold him." He turned to Lyon, who was mounted now. "As you go down the valley, watch for Private Krause's body. I'm sure he was taking Bessie Gordon that way. He wasn't too smart, but he was smart enough not to ride toward the enemy camp. If you find him, report at the fort so they can send an ambulance out to take him in."

Private Lyon left the camp at a lope and disappeared almost immediately in the darkness. Lane wasn't sure about the wisdom of sending Lyon for help. His presence here might have been more valuable. It would be at least a day, maybe two, before help would arrive. That would surely be too late for Stella and Bessie.

Now there was just Lane, Sergeant Dodson, and Private Voage to oppose Widlow's gang. And they had a prisoner to guard, besides. Private Voage had been given the job. Lane doubted if he'd be relieved of it now.

"Maybe we could suggest swapping prisoners," Dodson said. "I'm sure they'd like to have Turley back."

Lane shook his head. "I doubt it. If they thought much of Turley they wouldn't have left without checking to see if he was alive. Remember, they abandoned him."

Dodson chewed his lip and nodded. "Maybe that isn't such a good idea. We'll just have to wait for reinforcements."

"Can't you think any way but army?" Lane

said disgustedly. “Widlow has both those girls. He’s demanding that gold now or he’ll kill them. I don’t take that threat lightly. Before any reinforcements can get here, Widlow will have that gold or he’ll kill the girls.”

“What do you suggest?” Dodson demanded angrily.

“That we go after the girls ourselves. It’ll be dangerous and it may get them and us killed. But if we can’t find the gold, it will almost surely mean their death, anyway. How about it?”

“You’re talking my language now,” Dodson said. He glanced back at Voage, close to the prisoner. “We’ll have to leave Voage with Turley.”

“Two of us are enough. The more we have, the more likely we are to be discovered. We can’t overpower them so we have to outsmart them.”

“They’ll be watching for us,” Dodson said. “But it’s the best we can do unless we wait for reinforcements. Let’s go.”

Lane hesitated. “Wait a minute. Widlow stopped right in the middle of the canyon this afternoon. You know he won’t stay there, especially now that he has Stella, too. He’ll pick a place where we can’t find him. I think you had a good idea.”

Dodson frowned. “What idea?”

“Offering a trade of prisoners.”

“You just said he wouldn’t do that.”

“I don’t expect him to,” Lane said. “But if we write a note and make that offer, whoever picks up the note will have to deliver it to Widlow. We can follow him and locate the camp."

Dodson grinned. "Sharp thinking. I'll write the note."

They took the note to the rock where they'd found Widlow's note. Lane fired his gun in the air. Then he and Dodson turned back toward their camp. They went only a short distance, then slipped back to a spot where they could see the rock but not be seen themselves.

Lane was almost surprised at how soon a man appeared and picked up the note. He didn't even try to read it and Lane guessed that he couldn't read. So much the better. He'd have to take it to Widlow to find out what it said.

Lane and Dodson moved out well behind the man. Lane went ahead, moving as quietly as possible. Dodson stayed within following distance of Lane, but the messenger wasn't likely to hear any noise he made. The messenger went down the canyon for a way, met another man, and they went on together, finally cutting sharply into a small side canyon that Lane knew he would have missed in the darkness.

Dodson was close behind Lane when they turned into the small canyon. Lane stopped when he spotted a tiny campfire ahead. He'd found the camp. Dodson caught up with him. Lane whispered to the sergeant that he'd slip in and locate the girls and report back.

The darkness was an asset to Lane now. From a fallen rock, he peered over at the camp. He soon located the girls a short distance from the fire. He guessed Widlow didn't want them to overhear what he was saying to the others. Lane recognized Widlow and Bumbry at the fire. The stocky man, Medder, was there. He had just turned over the note that Dodson had written.

Lane had to search for a while to find the small gang member, Copo. He was just to one side of the spot where the girls were tied, settling himself against a rock. Apparently he had just taken over the job of guarding them. Lane slipped back and reported to Dodson and they made their plans.

"We'll have to eliminate the guard first without any noise," Dodson said.

Lane nodded. "He's leaning against a rock. I think I can sneak up behind that rock and rap him over the head with my gun barrel."

"If you can, that will take care of him," Dodson said. "Will the girls remain quiet when they see us?"

"I'm betting Stella will. I don't know about Bessie. I'll try to make sure Stella sees me first. Then maybe she can keep Bessie quiet."

Lane stole softly forward until he was within a few feet of the rock where Copo was sitting. Quietly he moved forward until he was behind the rock. Copo hadn't moved. Reaching out silently, Lane brought the barrel of his gun down hard along the side of Copo's head. The man grunted and slipped over on his side.

Lane's eyes flashed to the fire. Bumbry turned his head their way, but when he didn't see anything move, he turned back to his conversation with Widlow.

Lane slid quietly around the rock where he could see Stella. She saw him and her eyes widened, but she didn't make a sound.

"Keep Bessie quiet," he whispered.

He disappeared behind the rock while Stella whispered to Bessie. The men at the fire wouldn't notice anything unusual about that. Then Dodson moved past Lane and used his knife to make sure Copo didn't come to and shout a warning.

Lane had his own knife and used it to cut the ropes holding the girls' hands and feet. Widlow stood up and looked at the girls. Then he sent Medder over to make sure all was well. Lane tensed. This could quickly erupt into a battle and that was the one thing he and Dodson wanted to avoid. Even if they won the fight, the girls would almost surely get hit in the fray.

Medder came only a short distance and stopped. "Everything all right, Dorse?" he asked.

"Fine," Lane said softly.

Medder turned and went back to the fire. He wasn't any better at checking things than he was at reading, Lane decided. He saw Widlow throw the paper Dodson had sent into the fire. That was about what Lane had expected.

Now that Medder had checked, the men at the fire concentrated on their conversation without a glance at the prisoners. Lane took advantage of that to get the girls around the rock. Then he and Dodson hurried away, nobody talking or making any unnecessary noise.

They were out of the side pocket when they heard a shout behind them. Someone had noticed that the prisoners were gone. Another shout followed that. Lane guessed they had found Copo. They hurried up the valley toward their own camp where the horses were. He wished they had the horses now, but they couldn't have followed the messenger undetected if they'd had horses.

The pursuit was cautious as the outlaws tried to ferret out the escapees in the darkness. The fugitives were nearing their own camp when the outlaws caught a glimpse of them. They fired several shots their way. One bullet cut through Lane's sleeve and dug a furrow along his arm, but Lane couldn't worry about that now.

Lane motioned Dodson to take the girls on to the camp while he ran to one side. From there he fired twice at the outlaws. Lane was sure he hadn't hit anything, but it brought all three pursuers his way. As silently as a shadow, he ran along the canyon wall, then cut back toward the camp, losing his pursuers.

At the camp, Dodson had everything loaded ready for flight. Voage had Turley on a horse, hands tied to the saddle horn. Bessie and Stella were both on Stella's horse. Bessie's had been lost to the outlaws.

"Let's go east," Dodson said. "They'll expect us to go north toward the road to the fort."

Bessie was almost hysterical. Only Stella could keep her quiet. Then Stella saw the blood on Lane's arm and she almost lost control of herself. She slid off her horse and ran to him.

"Let me fix that," she said.

"Later when we get where we're not exposed," he said. "It's only a scratch."

"That's more than a scratch," Stella said, touching his arm tenderly.

But she went back to her horse and they rode east, going as quietly as they could. Lane couldn't understand the sudden concern in Stella. Nothing had upset her before. She hadn't even appeared greatly upset over being a prisoner. But she had lost her calmness over this little wound.

Dodson, riding ahead, found a small pocket that he said they could easily defend in case the outlaws found them. They rode into the tiny valley and dismounted. If Widlow didn't find them here, they could go on to the fort tomorrow morning.

Stella came straight to Lane and with a piece of

cloth, apparently ripped from her petticoat, she bound up the arm and stopped the bleeding. She seemed unduly concerned about it, Lane thought, but he liked the attention and said nothing. Bessie didn't even seem to notice that anyone had been wounded. Lane suspected her captivity had been hard on her.

Turley was making more noise than Dodson liked, claiming that he should be given his freedom in exchange for the information he had given the army. But Dodson made it clear that he had no intention of letting the man go until he was tried for his crimes.

Lane heard horses nearing their hideout and knew the outlaws had discovered they had come this way. The sounds stopped outside the little pocket. Lane wondered if they were guessing or if they knew they had turned in here.

A shot that ricocheted off a rock close to the mouth of the little pocket convinced Lane the outlaws knew they were here.

"You've had it now," Turley said almost gleefully. "Easy has you trapped."

"You're trapped with us," Lane said.

"He ain't going to shoot me," Turley said. "But you ain't getting out of here alive. Nobody crosses Easy Widlow and lives to tell about it."

"You think nobody can lick him?" Lane asked.

"I know they can't," Turley said confidently.

Lane would have to have that proved to him. But he also had to admit that they had backed themselves into a hole. They should have kept running.

X

Lane wished they had not holed up in this small pocket. Even though Widlow had only Bumbry and Medder with him, they could easily hold them here. One man could almost do that.

He didn't know what time it was, but he was sure it was nearing dawn. He wondered if they could break out of this trap before it got light.

"We need more men," Dodson said.

"We don't have them," Lane said. "We could use Voage up here."

"Can't afford to take him away from his guard post over Turley."

"Is it that important to you that Turley be given a trial at the fort?" Lane asked.

"That's what we're supposed to do with criminals like him when we catch them. I intend to do it."

"You didn't give Copo that chance."

"That was a battle," Dodson said stiffly. "Turley is a prisoner. He'll be treated like a prisoner."

During the war, Lane hadn't understood the way the army thought about some things. He still didn't understand it. A shot from the dark made him realize that Turley was a minor problem right now. They had to defend themselves from the outlaws who could move around as they pleased while those in the little pocket had little room to move.

Voage came up from the rear of the pocket. “Looks like you need help here,” he said.

“What about Turley?” Dodson demanded.

“He’s tied up good,” Voage said. “I think we can get out of this pocket by scaling the west wall.”

“Can’t take our horses,” Dodson said. “We must have our horses.”

“I reckon so,” Voage said, disappointment in his voice.

“You return to your post, Private,” Dodson said. “Lane and I will hold the line against the enemy.”

“The prisoner insists on talking to you,” Voage said. “He feels he should be released because he has cooperated with you and told you what he knows.”

“Those things will be recognized at his trial,” Dodson said. “You can tell him that.”

“He says he’d like to help us in the fight,” Voage said.

Dodson looked at Lane. “Do you believe that? I don’t.”

Lane recalled how Turley had taunted them just a few minutes before. He shook his head. “I wouldn’t trust him an inch.”

“Keep an eye on him,” Dodson said and Voage turned and headed back.

Lane picked a nest of boulders at one side of the mouth of the little canyon and got down among them. He'd make a small target there. He saw Dodson doing almost the same thing across the opening.

Lane realized that he could see farther than he could a few minutes before. Dawn was coming. He wasn't sure whether that would be to his advantage or not. The pocket Dodson had chosen would have been ideal for a hiding place if Widlow hadn't discovered they were in it. Now it was a trap.

A shot came from out front, apparently not aimed directly at anything. It was just a reminder that they were bottled up here.

"Any ideas how we're going to get out of here?" Lane asked Dodson.

"Not at the moment," Dodson admitted. "When it gets light enough that we can see where they're holed up, we may be able to concentrate our fire and drive them back."

Lane realized that if the cover was not too good out in the main valley, he and Dodson might have an advantage here in the little pocket where rocks had fallen and could be used as breastworks.

As the light got stronger, the firing increased. Then Lane's attention was pulled away from the battle as Voage came over to the mouth of the pocket.

"What are you doing here now?" Dodson demanded.

"The prisoner has escaped," Voage reported. "I thought he was tied securely."

"Well, he must be hiding somewhere in this canyon. He can't get far."

"I searched everywhere," Voage said. "I told you I thought we could climb out the side of this hole. I think Turley did just that."

"Didn't the girls see him?" Lane asked.

"No," Voage said. "I asked them first off. They hadn't noticed him at all. They'd been watching for the attack up here."

"Where will he go?" Dodson wondered.

"Probably back to Widlow," Lane said. "He seemed to think Widlow was invincible."

"Likely," Dodson agreed. "Well, Private, since you don't have a prisoner to guard, you can dig in here and help us hold off this bunch."

Voage looked for a rock big enough to hide behind and scooted down with his rifle to wait for a target to appear.

The light grew stronger and Lane searched for objects out in the valley. He didn't see many rocks out there and no trees. This side canyon they had turned up did not have a creek in it and there was little vegetation other than grass.

The guns out in front picked up the tempo as the light strengthened. The bullets were having little effect. Lane fired at the gun flashes a few times, but mainly he kept his head down.

He was surprised and shocked when Stella suddenly appeared in the rocks beside him.

"I want to help whip those thieves," she said.

"There are three of us," Lane said. "We can handle them. I don't want you to get hurt and you may if you stay here."

Lane heard a wail back in the pocket and turned his attention that way. Stella turned her head, too.

"Something wrong with Bessie?" Lane asked.

"She's almost hysterical," Stella said. "I can't keep her calm."

"You can do us the most good by staying with her," Lane said. "I'll feel much better with you back there, anyway."

"I want to do something to help here," Stella said. But her eyes kept darting back toward the wailing sound. "I'll have to help Bessie now," she said finally. "If you need another gun, I can handle one."

"I'll remember that," Lane promised and watched Stella duck into the back part of the little canyon. He knew he'd never have been able to concentrate on fighting if Stella was exposed to danger here.

"Not much cover out there," Dodson said. "Let's make it hot for them."

The three rifles at the mouth of the little canyon opened up with a rapid fire. The men who had moved fairly close to the pocket suddenly took to their heels, dodging to the east where some rocks offered better protection.

"If we can drive them out of those rocks, we can get everybody out of here," Lane said. "Let's go."

He moved up to the corner of the pocket and took careful aim at the rocks where Widlow's men were. The dawn light was good enough now for fairly accurate shooting. It was also good enough to show Lane that there were four men out there and he was sure he recognized Fel Turley as one of the four.

Concentrated fire drove Widlow's men out of the rocks and they retreated to a jumble of rocks farther up the canyon. Lane turned to Dodson.

"Get the girls and horses and move out of here. Leave my horse so I can follow. Right now, I'll keep Widlow's outfit snug in those rocks up there. They're too far away to bother you as you leave."

Lane picked a big rock up the canyon a ways and scooted toward it, using the rocks and a slight curve in the canyon wall to shield him until he was in position. Then he fired at any head that bobbed up. He barely looked behind him, but he was aware when the horses left. Voage dodged up beside Lane and added his rifle to the barrage keeping Widlow's men down in their rocks.

"Gave Bessie the army horse that we'd been carting Turley around on," Voage said. "The sergeant is heading back to the main valley with the girls. He says he'll find a safe spot to hide and watch for us when we come."

"Good," Lane said. "We'll try to hold them in those rocks long enough for Dodson to have time to find a good place."

It wasn't a difficult job holding Widlow's men in the rocks. Each time one poked up his head, either Lane or Voage would take a shot at it. Lane was sure they hadn't inflicted any wounds on the outlaws, but they were keeping them effectively bottled up.

Finally Lane suggested. "Let's give them a good barrage, then get out of here. Make sure they don't see you retreat to the horses."

Lane fired several shots, took time to reload, then, ducking low, headed back to the spot where the horses were waiting. The little curve in the canyon's wall kept them out of sight of Widlow's men. They mounted and headed west toward the main valley, hugging the wall, hoping they could keep out of sight.

They reached the main valley without any sign of pursuit and turned north. There the valley slanted down rather rapidly toward the Platte. They had passed the wrecked wagons before Dodson waved to them from a side gully.

It wasn't the sort of hiding place Lane would have picked. But it could prove to be a better place because Widlow might overlook it, too.

It wasn't really a camp, just a place to hide. Lane's first reaction was to make a dash for Fort McPherson before Widlow caught up.

He doubted, however, if they could keep ahead of the outlaws. Personally he was in no hurry to get away from them. He still had a score to settle with Bumbry and Widlow because of his brother's death.

Lane found Bessie calmed down at last. She didn't look like the frivolous girl who had tried to coax Lane into helping her get some of the gold. He wondered if she could tell him now what she and Krause had done.

"What happened to the gold you and Krause had?" Lane asked.

"Widlow got it," Bessie said softly. "They shot Pud, then took our horses and everything we had, including the pouch of gold."

Lane turned to Stella. "Can you pay off the banker with what you have left?"

Stella shook her head. "Pa arranged for just enough gold to pay off the mortgage. Knowing now where the foreman put it, I can see why he didn't put in more."

Lane nodded. He understood what a job it must have been to split that axle and hollow out the cavities for those pouches, without the driver of the wagon knowing about it.

"Looks like we'll have to get that gold that Widlow stole from Bessie," Lane said.

Stella agreed. "But how are we going to get it?"

"I have some things to settle with Widlow and Bumbry," Lane said. "I don't know how I'm going to manage it, but that gold will be an objective, too."

Sergeant Dodson came up. "Let's get on the road before Widlow shows up. If we hurry, we can be back at the fort tonight."

"We have to get that gold Widlow stole from Bessie," Stella said.

Dodson shook his head. "The army is interested in saving lives, not gold. We've got a chance now to beat Widlow out of this valley. I thought he'd be hot on our trail, but he's not. Let's go."

"Go ahead," Stella said. "I'm staying till I get that gold."

Dodson stared at her in disbelief. "Turley has escaped and joined with Widlow. That makes four of them. We have only three men. How do you expect us to whip that gang?"

"I'm not interested in whipping the gang, just getting my gold back, so I can pay off the mortgage," Stella said.

"I'd like to hear your battle plan for doing that," Dodson said scathingly.

Stella ignored him and turned to Lane. "Maybe Widlow will leave now and we won't get the chance to recover that gold."

Lane looked at Bessie. "Does Widlow know how much more gold there is?"

Bessie nodded. "Ken Sanford told him there were four bags of gold."

"Then I'm betting he won't leave as long as he thinks he has a chance of getting it all." Lane turned to Dodson. "I reckon I'll stay with the girls and try to get their gold back."

Dodson scowled. Whatever he did was not going to be according to army protocol. Finally he nodded.

"It's against my better judgment, but Private Voage and I will stay, too. Together we'll have a much better chance against Widlow. I would like to recapture Turley and corral the rest of the outlaws, too."

Dodson stationed Voage at the end of the gully to guard against a surprise attack from Widlow's gang while he and Lane and the girls tried to devise a plan to recapture the gold.

Now that it was settled that they would stay and try to get the gold Widlow had stolen, Stella turned her attention to Lane's wound, unwrapping the bandage she had put on, washing the wound carefully, and re-bandaging it. Lane was seeing a tender side of Stella he hadn't known existed. He had to admit he liked it.

When Stella had finished with the bandage, she looked at Lane. "I want you to keep the gold for me," she said simply.

"Why? They can get it from me as well as anyone. Besides, none of us know where it is."

Stella smiled. “I didn’t want anyone to find it and I didn’t want it to get far from us.” She went to Private Voage’s pack and reached into his raincoat, bringing out the three pouches of gold. “I’m sure Private Voage didn’t know he was carrying the gold. If Widlow should capture us, he’ll search me and my things first. He won’t suspect you of having it.”

Reluctantly Lane accepted the gold, hiding it a few feet from his own bedroll. He was amazed at Stella giving him custody of the pouches. It was the first sign he’d seen of her depending on someone else for anything.

For the moment, things seemed quiet and safe. Dodson called Lane and the girls over to the place where he was sitting on a rock.

“If we’re going to try to outsmart Widlow, we’ve got to do some hard thinking. Widlow is a sharp one. He wouldn’t be running free yet if he wasn’t. You’re the one who wants to try to get that gold from him. Do you have any plan on how to do it?”

Stella shook her head. “I only know I have to get that gold or lose my mine and ranch. I don’t intend to lose them.”

“It takes more than good intentions,” Dodson said. “If Private Lyon gets back with reinforcements, then we can hunt Widlow down and attack his outfit. But the three of us are hardly enough to launch an attack.”

"We could try sneaking in and surprising him," Lane suggested. "But it won't be as easy as it was to get the girls away from him. We could see where they were. We'll have no idea where he's hiding the gold."

"We'll have to capture Widlow himself," Dodson said. "I think he'll carry that gold on his person. He's too self-important to allow anyone else to handle it."

"You're probably right about that," Stella said. "But how do we capture him?"

Suddenly their discussion was exploded by a rifle shot. Lane and Dodson jumped up.

"Voage must have seen somebody," Dodson said.

Lane was already running toward Voage. Before he was halfway there, he saw that Private Voage was down on the ground. It hadn't been Voage's rifle they had heard. Apparently Widlow's outfit had located their hiding place.

Lane saw a man dodging along the valley wall leading into the gully. He fired a quick shot at him. Behind him, Dodson also sent a shot that way. The man ducked behind some rocks. It wasn't good protection, but it was more protection than Lane and Dodson had.

Suddenly there was a scream behind Lane. He wheeled. There was a man in camp and he was wrestling with Stella. Lane was sure the man he and Dodson had pinned down was Fel Turley.

He couldn't see at first glance who had grabbed Stella.

"Get that fellow in the rocks," Lane said. "I'm going to help Stella."

Running back, he saw that the outlaw there was Nick Medder, the one who had knocked him out with a rock. He must be trying to force Stella to tell where the gold was.

Lane gave no more thought to Medder's intentions. With a final leap, he hit the man, knocking him down and dragging Stella down with them. Medder twisted to face Lane.

Lane yanked Medder away from Stella, who scrambled to her feet. Medder turned his full attention to Lane. Lane knew this was not the way he should fight a man like Medder. A standing fist fight would give Lane an advantage because of his reach, but a rough and tumble dogfight would be to Medder's advantage.

Then Lane thought of Stella, who had been fighting Medder, and his fury at the outlaw's nerve sent a surge of strength through him. For the moment, he was a match for the heavyset outlaw. He forced the man down and was getting the best of him.

Then Medder twisted around and came up with a knife. Lane knew he was no match for Medder and a knife.

XI

Thinking of Stella and the way Nick Medder had been manhandling her, Lane found additional strength. The sight of the knife moving slowly toward him added to his desperation. He got his hand on Medder's wrist and a new struggle of strength began.

Lane saw Stella circling them, trying to get close enough to kick the knife away. He was sure she'd be hurt if she got involved. He had to conquer Medder before that happened.

Lunging to one side and twisting Medder's wrist with all the strength he had, Lane tried to wrench the knife out of Medder's grasp, but he couldn't do it. He did manage to turn Medder partly over and, with an additional jerk, he turned his wrist until the knife blade was pointed away from himself.

Lane jerked to one side to escape Medder and yanked him over. Nick Medder crashed down on his own knife. He flayed around for a moment, then lay still.

Lane got to his feet, panting, his arms and hands shaking from the exertion of the last few seconds.

"Is—is he dead?" Bessie asked fearfully.

"At least he won't be bothering us for a while," Lane said.

He heard Dodson still shooting and remembered that Medder wasn't the only one here. Lane wheeled toward the mouth of the gully.

"What about this man?" Stella asked.

Lane looked down and turned Medder over. He pulled the knife free and dropped it next to the rock where they'd been fighting. The knife slid under the edge of the rock. A look at the set stare of the outlaw's eyes told him he wouldn't be needing the knife anymore.

"Just move back where you don't have to look at him," Lane suggested to Stella and Bessie. "I've got to help the sergeant."

He got to the end of the gully just as Dodson stood up. Lane saw a man dodging away, going toward the top of the valley.

"Missed him?" Lane asked.

"I think I hit him," Dodson said. "But I didn't stop him."

"Did you see who it was?" Lane asked.

"It was Turley," Dodson said. "I sure wanted to get him when I saw who it was."

"What made him run?"

"At least I can take credit for that," Dodson said. "I was making it hot for him. I've got to see what happened to Voage."

Lane went with the sergeant to the spot where Voage had been standing guard. Voage was shot in the side, but he was still conscious. Dodson knelt beside him and examined the wound.

"Is it that bad?" Voage whispered.

Dodson shook his head. "You'll pull through. We'll stop the bleeding. Then I'll take you to the fort. They can fix you up there."

"I didn't see anybody," Voage said.

"We got one of them," Lane said. "The other one is hit."

Stella came from farther back in the gully. "Can I help?" she asked.

"What about Bessie?" Lane asked.

"I took her back a ways and got her quieted down. I think she'll be all right." She looked at Voage. "I knew Private Voage had been hit and I thought I might be able to help."

"You sure can," Dodson said. "We have to stop the bleeding so I can take him to the fort hospital."

Lane saw that Dodson was skilled in bandaging wounds and Stella was a real help to him. Lane was unneeded.

Just then shots echoed out in the valley, muffled by distance. Lane wheeled that way and Dodson looked up from his work.

"Who would be shooting now?" Dodson asked. "And what at?"

"Can't think of anybody out there except Widlow's gang," Lane said. "I'll check on it."

"Be careful," Dodson warned. "There's not much of any place out there to hide."

Lane nodded. "I know."

Stella stood up. "Does it make any difference who they are shooting at as long as it's not us?"

"Maybe not. But it's a good idea to know what is going on."

Dodson's face suddenly brightened. "Maybe Private Lyon is back with reinforcements."

Lane shook his head. "Not enough time yet. Besides, Lyon would bring in the troops from the river. Those shots were up the valley."

Dodson's face fell. "Reckon so."

Lane moved out to the mouth of the gully. There was nothing in sight out in the valley. He disliked leaving the security of the gully, but he needed to know what had happened.

It could be important to their survival. He wasn't fooling himself into thinking that Widlow and Bumbry might give up the chase for the gold the Gordon sisters had.

Lane was moving slowly along the edge of the valley, hoping to get a look around the curve without being seen when a man stumbled around the curve and came toward him.

Lane had his gun in his hand and he centered it on the man, but he didn't shoot. The man was weaving like a drunk man and Lane could see the blood on the front of his shirt. It was Fel Turley. Lane's next thought was that Dodson had been more accurate with his shooting than he had thought.

Lane backed against the slope of the valley and

waited. Even this could be a trick, he thought. He didn't put anything past Bumbry or Widlow. Turley staggered closer to Lane, but then he tottered and fell ten feet away.

Lane waited for him to get up, but he didn't. Cautiously he went to the fallen outlaw. He saw when he got there Turley wasn't putting on a show of being seriously wounded. He was dying.

Kneeling beside Turley, Lane rolled him over.

"Did Dodson hit you this hard?" he asked.

"Wasn't Dodson," Turley said. "It was Easy."

"Widlow?" Lane said.

Turley nodded his head slightly.

"Why would he shoot you?"

"For trying to get the gold instead of letting him get it."

That still didn't make sense to Lane. "Why should he care whether you got it or he did?"

"Medder," Turley murmured. "Medder—him and me—were going to take . . . the gold and . . . and run."

"Oh," Lane said, seeing it clearly now.

Turley coughed weakly, then gasped and was still. Lane got up quickly. If Widlow was furious enough to shoot Turley, he might also follow him to make sure he was dead. But there was no one in sight.

Lane considered his next move. If Stella was to save her mine and ranch, she had to have the gold that Widlow had taken from Bessie. And there was still Lane's own personal vengeance. Bumbry had betrayed everyone on that wagon train. He had to take responsibility for the deaths of all those men, including his brother, Chris. Widlow was little better, maybe just as bad. Lane wouldn't rest easy until he had settled the score with both of them. In the process, he'd try to get Stella's gold for her.

He glanced back at the gully where Dodson and the girls waited. Then he turned and moved onward. Stopping where he could see most of the upper valley, he studied it carefully for some sign of Widlow or Bumbry. But the area appeared deserted.

Lane considered going into the upper valley and trying to flush out the outlaws. But he knew his chances of surviving if he did find them were mighty slim. They'd see him before he saw them.

Slowly he turned back toward the gully. Widlow must know the soldiers had their camp close by or he wouldn't have known what Turley and Medder had tried to do. He'd also know that the shots he'd fired at Turley would have been heard in the camp. So he'd expect someone to investigate. If Lane moved up the valley, Widlow would be waiting for him somewhere.

At the gully he found Dodson still with Voage, and Stella was there, too. They had a bandage made of a shirt wrapped tightly around Voage. It appeared that the bleeding had stopped.

"What was it?" Dodson asked.

"Turley had been shot by Widlow. Seems Widlow resented Turley and Medder trying to steal the gold. They were going to run out on Widlow. Widlow found out and he killed Turley for his part in it."

"At least there are only two of them now to give us trouble," Dodson said. "But I guess they've won the battle, anyway."

"Giving up?" Lane asked.

"Got to get Voage to the post hospital. I think he's got a good chance of making it if I can get him to the doctor. He won't if we leave him here. It's like they told us in the war. If you kill a man, you take one out of the fight. But if you wound one, you take two men out of the fight—the wounded man and the man who takes him back to the doctor."

Lane nodded. "You're going to take him back yourself?"

"Got to. Nobody else to do it. I don't think he can ride a horse, though. Is there one good set of running gears among those wrecked wagons?"

"I think so," Lane said. "But he'll need more than running gears to ride on."

"I figure we can find a part of a box to set on the running gears so I can take him in," Dodson said. "I'll take the girls in with me. We can use two of the horses to pull the wagon. Surely there's enough harness up there for that."

"We'd better all go when we try to fix up a rig," Lane said. "Widlow can figure quickly where we left the girls if he sees us without them."

"You're right," Dodson said. "Let's get at it. Voage needs help as soon as possible."

"Wait a minute," Stella said. "Lane, you'll have to get the gold. If we leave it here, Widlow might find it."

Lane nodded. "You're right. Why don't you bring it with you? Then you'll have it when you start for the fort."

"I can't go," Stella said. "I've got to get that gold Widlow stole from Bessie."

"If the sergeant goes back, you'll have to go," Lane said. "There will be nobody to protect you."

Stella's face fell. "If everybody goes, I'll have to, I suppose."

"I'm not going," Lane said. "I have a score to settle with Bumbry. And there is the chance that I'll get that gold Widlow stole. But I can do that better alone."

"I can't take that gold out with me," Stella said. "Widlow will probably hold us up. He can't help seeing us go."

Lane recognized the logic in that. Widlow couldn't miss what was going on. He'd see the girls on the wagon and guess the gold was there, too.

"We'll hide it somewhere," he said. "Then

when I come in, I'll bring it. If I don't make it, you can come back and get it yourself."

Lane went back and got the gold while Dodson got the horses and Bessie. Lane and Stella went in search of a place where they could hide the gold so no one would find it until they were ready to take it out.

Not far below the gully, they found a bluff that stuck out from the side of the valley. The rocks were crumbling off the bluff into a pile below. It was a natural place to hide something. Too natural, Lane knew.

The rocks that had tumbled off the cliff in years past were scattered around and Lane saw one twenty yards down the valley from the bluff. It was half covered with grass. He went to it and gently lifted it. Carefully he scooped out a handful of dirt and carried it back to the rock pile. Repeating this, he hollowed out a spot where the three pouches of gold could nestle without making a lump above the level of the ground. Then, very carefully, he moved the rock back into its original place. There was no bulge or even any sign that the rock had been moved. Stella checked to make sure there was no dirt spilled around to indicate the rock had been disturbed.

"They shouldn't find that," Lane said. He looked around. "This seems to be about the only rock outcropping along here. We shouldn't have any trouble finding this when we want it."

"This is safer than trying to take it out on the wagon," Stella said. She looked at Lane. "If I can't stay to help you, I wish you'd come, too. I'm not sure trying to get that gold from Widlow is worth the risk you're taking."

"I told you, it's not just the gold. I have personal reasons for staying and I'd stay whether there was any gold to recover or not."

Stella didn't take her eyes off him. "I know you're going to look for that gold," she said.

"Well," he admitted, "if I see it, I'll pick it up. You can be sure of that."

Back at the gully, Dodson was ready to move. "I'm going to take Voage out where we can see him from the wagons," he said. "We can't move him up to the wagons without a stretcher, but we can keep an eye on him as we work."

Lane helped him lift Voage and lay him on the grass out in the valley. Then he and Dodson, Stella and Bessie headed toward the wagons, leading all the horses.

Checking the four wagons, they found two of the running gears were broken. The outlaws had done a thorough job of tearing up everything trying to find the gold. Lane found one set of running gears that seemed intact except for a broken wheel. They took a wheel off another wagon. Then they found a box that had the bed still relatively intact. One side and the rear endgate were gone. But they could use the bed for Voage to lie on during the trip to the fort.

Lane kept watch for Widlow and Bumbry while Dodson looked for some harness that was still usable. Most of it was badly tangled.

The saddle horses didn't take kindly to a collar and harness, but there was no choice. The animals, gentled through much work, finally accepted the strange apparatus and pulled ahead when Dodson led them.

They moved the patched-up conveyance over to the spot where Voage lay and loaded him on the bed of the wagon.

"You'd better go with us," Dodson said. "I hate to leave a man out here alone where outlaws are at home."

"You know I've got to stay," Lane said.

"I'll bring help back as soon as I can," Dodson promised. "If we meet Lyon with reinforcements, I'll let him take Voage on in and I'll come back with the soldiers."

Lane nodded although he was sure that would be too late to help him. Once the soldiers were gone, he'd have to face Widlow and Bumbry alone. They wouldn't wait for reinforcements to come.

Stella came over. "I still wish you'd come with us," she said.

"I'll see you at the fort," he said with more confidence than he really felt.

Bessie came over and gave him an impulsive

hug. "You're an angel to do this for us," she said.

"I don't want to be an angel for a while, at least," he said, grinning.

With all of them loaded on the wagon and Dodson driving, Lane had second thoughts. Widlow and Bumbry surely must have been watching what they were doing. If Lane stayed behind, they'd know what he was going to try, and he'd likely be ambushed before he had time to do anything. Mounting his horse, he rode along behind the wagon as it went down the valley.

Only when they left the valley and turned east along the road to Fort McPherson did he rein up. With a wave of his hand to them, he turned his horse back. He hoped Widlow was convinced by now that he was going to Fort McPherson with Dodson.

Lane rode into the valley and stopped. For half an hour he listened. If Dodson was held up, there might be shots. Lane felt better as each minute passed and nothing but silence came back to him. Maybe Dodson had gotten through without being held up. In that case, Widlow and Bumbry wouldn't know that Lane hadn't gone to the fort with Dodson.

He knew he didn't have long to get Stella's gold from Widlow if she was to have time to get it to the Omaha bank before the deadline. He had to find Widlow and Bumbry, and he had to have a plan. He couldn't hope to face them on even terms and get the gold Widlow had.

He decided he'd go back to the gully where they had holed up this morning. He needed time to think and they'd never look for him there, even if they suspected he had stayed behind.

He rode into the little gully a while later. He had to come up with a plan to trap the outlaws.

He had barely dismounted when he was aware of a sudden movement behind him. Wheeling, he reached for his gun. But they were too close, Bumbry and Widlow. They had outsmarted him in guessing he would come back here.

Before Lane could get his gun out of the holster, one man jabbed a gun in his middle while the other one slammed his gun barrel over his head.

Lane's last thought before everything blacked out was that he'd been a fool to think he could outwit Easy Widlow.

XII

Consciousness came back slowly to Lane. He thought he was climbing a long hill with flashes of fire leaping up at him at every step. He wasn't going to make it to the top.

Then those flashes of fire became pains in his head and he tried to reach up to rub them away. It was then that he became conscious enough to realize that his hands were tied behind his back. He tried to move his feet. They were tied, too.

He stopped trying to move and let his mind clear. He remembered riding into the gully, feeling secure. Then after dismounting, he had turned to face a gun and the sharp stab of pain as he was hit on the head.

He wondered why they had knocked him out and tied him up instead of killing him. They obviously wanted him dead. Maybe they wanted something from him before they killed him.

"Ain't he come to yet?" one of the men said a short distance away.

Lane wasn't sure just which one of them had spoken. He wasn't going to open an eye to see. That would tell them he was back in the real world.

"You sure you didn't kill him?" the same voice said.

"I didn't kill him. Look at him. You can see he's breathing. He's probably faking it now."

Lane heard steps as someone moved away, then, after a short time, came back. He wasn't aware of what was going on until he felt the cold splash of water in his face. He would still have feigned unconsciousness if some of the water hadn't gotten into his mouth and choked him. His coughing brought him to a sitting position.

"That's more like it," Bumbry growled, crouching in front of Lane. "I thought you was faking it. Now I want to know where that gold is."

Lane stalled, letting his mind clear some more. How did Bumbry know the girls didn't have it? Maybe they didn't even know that the rest of his party was gone. Dodson had thought they had given Widlow and Bumbry the slip when they left, but Lane hadn't considered that even a possibility. They had been out in the valley too long rigging up that wagon from the pieces left from the massacre to be ignored. Then that wagon had not gone quietly down the valley, especially with horses pulling it that were used to the saddle, not collar and harness.

Lane tried to keep his face blank. Maybe Bumbry would think he was still addled. Lane wasn't entirely sure that he wasn't. He couldn't understand how he could be in this situation. Why had Widlow and Bumbry set this trap for him at this place? How had they come to the conclusion that he would come back here?

Bumbry slapped Lane across the face. "Come out of it," he shouted. "Where is that gold?"

Lane let his mouth sag open and stared at Bumbry. "What gold?" he finally mumbled, mushing the words.

"He ain't back with us yet," Widlow said. "We've got time."

"I ain't so sure," Bumbry said. "When that sergeant gets back to the fort, he's liable to come roaring back here with a troop of cavalry. We'd better be long gone when that happens."

"It will take him a while to get that old patched-up wagon to the fort. Then he's going to want to see what the doc says about that wounded soldier. Then it takes time for army orders to work down to the ranks, you know."

"I know it better than you do," Bumbry growled. "I was in the war, you know. I wasn't running with guerrillas through the war."

"Nothing wrong with what I was doing," Widlow snapped testily. "We did our share just as much as you did. We learned in a hurry that you couldn't depend on the regulars to do anything right. By the time they passed information all the way up to the top brass and the orders worked their way back down to the soldiers who were to carry them out, it was too late most of the time. That's why we worked as guerrillas. I figure it will take a long time to get a troop organized to come out looking for us."

"You do your figuring; I'll do mine," Bumbry said. "Either way, the quicker we get that gold and get out of here, the better off we are."

"I'll agree to that," Widlow said. "But you ain't going to get any valuable information out of him till he comes around so he can think."

"He can think right now," Bumbry growled.

"Doesn't sound like it. That wallop you gave him may have made an idiot of him."

Bumbry swore. "The only idiots will be us if we don't make him talk right away."

Lane listened to the argument and realized that they knew more than he had thought. He saw that it was almost dark. How long had he been out? Then he remembered it had been late in the afternoon when he rode in here. He had waited a long time down at the end of the valley to make sure the wagon had not been stopped by the outlaws. He had heard nothing to indicate that it had.

Still, if the outlaws had known what was going on, why hadn't they stopped and searched the wagon? Everything was mixed up in his mind. Maybe he was a little addled.

Bumbry turned back to Lane, staring at him closely. Lane tried to look the part of a simpleton. He knew that as soon as Bumbry was sure he had regained his senses, the questions would be demanding and answers of some kind would have to be forthcoming.

Bumbry slapped Lane on both sides of the face. “Come out of it!” he snapped. “Where is that gold?”

Lane saw that he wasn’t going to be able to stall much longer. “What gold?” he mumbled.

“You know what gold I’m talking about,” Bumbry growled. “The gold that the Gordon girls had.”

“They must have it,” he muttered.

“Don’t tell me that,” Bumbry said. “We stopped that wagon and searched everything. They didn’t have it.”

Lane allowed the surprise to show in his face. “Where did you stop the wagon?”

“Ah, you’re coming to life now.” Bumbry seemed to relish the moment. “We caught up with them just after they turned down the valley toward the fort,” he said. “They didn’t have the gold.”

“Why didn’t you ask them where it was?”

“Oh, we did,” Bumbry said. “The only thing that stubborn girl would say was that you didn’t have it.”

Lane glanced from Bumbry to Widlow, who had come over close to his partner. “And you don’t believe her?”

Bumbry nodded. “We believe her now. We searched you, too, and you don’t have it. The one thing that girl didn't say was that you didn't know where it is."

"Maybe you asked the wrong girl," Lane said.

"We asked the younger one, too, but she said she didn't know anything about it, then went into hysterics. It was the stubborn one who knew."

Lane found it hard not to believe Bumbry. He said they had stopped the wagon. Apparently they had done it without firing a shot. That probably meant no one was hurt and he was glad of that. But if they held up the wagon down the valley, they must have taken a shortcut back here.

"If she wouldn't tell you what she did with it, what makes you think she told me?" Lane asked.

"She would have told somebody. The sergeant didn't know and I don't think the younger girl knew. So you'd better remember where it is."

Bumbry slapped Lane harder than before, then stared at him to see if he was going to say anything. Widlow bent closer to him, too.

"I don't think you're going to pound it out of him," Widlow said.

"We can't wait till he starves enough to tell us," Bumbry shot back.

"I know that," Widlow said. "There are faster ways than that. We'll keep him here till he tells us where it is."

"What if I don't know?" Lane asked.

"That's going to be too bad for you," Widlow

said with a shrug. "The world can get along without you."

Lane didn't take the threat lightly. He knew both of these men could kill without any compunction.

"Can you find some wood, Jud?" Widlow asked.

"There ain't much dry wood," Bumbry growled. "I didn't see any dead branches on those cottonwoods."

"Then pick up a couple of bushels of buffalo chips."

"What do you want them for?" Bumbry asked.

"I want them!" Widlow snapped disgustedly. "What does anybody want buffalo chips for? Go get them. We're going to have a fire."

"Two bushels?" Bumbry asked, scowling.

"We're going to have a hot fire. Now get going."

"I ain't no kid," Bumbry grunted. "Picking up chips is kids' work."

"And you're just the kid to do it," Widlow said.

"If you want those chips, go get them yourself," Bumbry said.

"You're going to get them," Widlow said softly. "If you want to argue about it, that's fine. I can finish this job now by myself."

Lane watched the expression on Bumbry's face. He wasn't in the habit of taking orders, only handing them out. But he was going to take this one. Growling like an aggravated bear, he went to his saddlebags and brought out a big gunny sack.

"I can't see out there in the dark," he grumbled, stopping and staring at Widlow.

"You're the one who said we couldn't wait," Widlow said.

Lane hoped the argument would come to a head. If one of the two was eliminated, it would improve his chances a little. But as long as he was wound up in these ropes, a child could control him. He didn't have to have a map drawn for him to know what was in Widlow's mind. A hot fire and a heated iron on a bare foot had forced many a man to reveal all the information he knew. Lane wondered if he might not tell rather than suffer that torture.

Bumbry glared at Widlow for a minute. Then, clutching the sack, he turned out into the dark, grumbling like a tormented bull. Widlow came closer to Lane and looked at him speculatively.

"Want to tell me where the gold is now?" he asked softly. "You can avoid a lot of grief if you do."

"You have to know something before you can tell it," Lane said. "That stubborn girl, as Bumbry calls her, didn't share her information with anyone."

Widlow rubbed his chin as if considering the veracity of what Lane was saying. Then he got a short rope and rolled Lane over on his stomach. Jerking his feet up against his back, he tied the rope between the ankle ropes and the wrist ropes, making Lane totally helpless.

"I'm going to get some sleep," he said. "I don't want you running off. We'll see what a hot foot will do to your memory. If you don't know, we won't lose anything by burning your feet."

Lane watched Widlow go over and stretch out in his blankets. Lane figured he was as good as dead whether he told or not.

When Lane was sure that Widlow was asleep, he struggled against the ropes, but he could barely move his body and he certainly could do nothing to untie the ropes. He hadn't found any ray of hope when he heard Bumbry coming back to camp. Lane pretended to be asleep when the man stamped in.

Bumbry had the sack over his shoulder and it appeared to be about full. Lane was surprised that Bumbry could find that many buffalo chips as dark as it was.

Bumbry stamped over to Widlow's bedroll, but there he stopped. Widlow stirred.

"I got 'em. Want to start the fire now?"

Widlow grunted sleepily. "We can't see to find the gold even if he tells us where it is," he mumbled. "We'll wait till morning. He ain't going nowhere."

Bumbry swore. "You had me chase all over

the valley in the dark, gathering chips, and now you're going to wait till morning to start the fire!"

"That's what I said," Widlow said. "Go to sleep. You're tired."

Lane could see the faint glint of the starlight on the gun Widlow had pulled out from under his blanket. Bumbry spun around without a word and went to his own blankets.

Lane was getting a reprieve that he hadn't expected, but he didn't know what good it would do him. Thinking about the torture to come was almost as bad as facing it. He knew Dodson couldn't get back with help before another day and that would be too late for him. Lane couldn't depend on Private Lyon showing up with reinforcements. Somehow he felt that Dodson had given up on Lyon bringing help. If Lane was going to escape this trap, he had to do it himself.

He tested the ropes again. There was no give to any of them. It would take a lot of slack if he were going to reach a knot with his fingers.

Suddenly a new thought struck him. He was in the same camp where he had killed Medder. Apparently Widlow and Bumbry had done something with the body because he was lying almost where Medder had died. Lane remembered dropping the knife here and it had slid under the edge of the rock. Could it possibly be there yet?

Hunching himself over against the boulder, he

squirmed around until his fingers were against the rock. He couldn't be sure he was on the right side of the rock to find the knife. Nor could he be sure Widlow or Bumbry hadn't found the knife when they moved the body.

His fingers probed under the edge of the rock and found nothing. He hunched himself a few inches along the edge of the rock and searched again.

It was on the fourth stop that his fingers touched the blade of the knife. Hope surged up in him for the first time. The weapon was there. Now he had to twist it around until he could use it.

It took several minutes to get the knife worked out of its hiding place, then another minute to get the handle into his hand. Twice he cut himself on the blade as he tried to work it through his hands until he could grip the handle.

Just as he gripped the handle, the blade hit the rock and the sharp ping sounded as loud to Lane as a rifle shot. He watched the two sleeping figures. Bumbry rolled over, but he soon quieted down again.

The only rope Lane could reach with the blade was the one tying the ropes on his ankles to the ropes on his wrists. He started sawing on that. It seemed to him that it took forever.

When the rope finally parted and his legs could straighten out, relief swept over him. The cramps in his legs eased. It also freed his arms enough that he could move them up and down. Slowly Lane twisted the knife until he got it between his wrists.

He began sawing on those ropes. Several times the knife slipped and he cut the skin on his wrists. Blood ran down onto his fingers, making it very hard to hold the knife steady.

Just when he felt he was making good progress on the rope holding his wrists together, the slippery thing slid from his fingers and clattered against the rock.

Lane pulled his feet back against his back as they had been before he cut the rope and lay still, waiting to see if either of the two men had been roused out of his sleep by the noise. Widlow didn't move, but Bumbry did. Apparently he was not in as deep a sleep as Widlow.

Lane almost held his breath as he waited to see if Bumbry would get up to investigate. He did rise up on one elbow and stare in the direction of Lane, but after a minute, he closed his eyes and was still.

Lane felt around cautiously for the knife and finally got it in his hands again. The handle was slippery with half-dried blood, but Lane gripped it as tightly as he could with numb fingers and began sawing once more. The knife slipped away from him again but made no noise this time because it fell on the ground.

Lane struggled to get the knife again and

finally managed to saw the last strand of the rope in two. His hands were free. Quickly he then cut the ropes holding his ankles.

He struggled to stand up. His feet were numb and his legs almost refused to work. He toppled against the rock and the knife clanged against it. Righting himself, he looked at the two sleeping outlaws. Only, now Bumbry was not sleeping. He was sitting up, staring around.

Lane was on his feet. He tried to run, still gripping the knife, but his legs almost refused to budge. He was hobbling as bad as a broken-legged steer.

Bumbry yelled and rolled out of his blankets. Lane hobbled away, the numbness leaving his legs as he pounded circulation back into them with his running.

A gun roared behind Lane, and he felt the bullet tear through his arm.

XIII

Lane wasn't sure how bad the wound was, but he knew it wasn't fatal. It seemed to lend power to his legs and he ran faster, his strength returning with every step.

More shots came his way but none hit him. Once out of the gully, he turned up the valley. He was sure they would expect him to head toward the Platte. He had escaped from the hands of the outlaws for the moment, but he was far from out of danger.

His only weapon was the knife that he had used to cut the ropes binding him. They had stripped him of his gun and gunbelt while he was unconscious. Lane had no idea where his horse was. In fact, he hadn't seen any horses in the camp when he came to. Evidently the outlaws had staked their horses out somewhere to graze.

If he could find his horse, he'd make a dash for it. But he had no idea where the horses were and he certainly had no time to look for them.

His arm was beginning to throb. Lane placed a hand over the wound and it came away dripping with blood. He'd have to find someplace where he could stop and try to staunch the bleeding. The way it was going, it would soon weaken him.

Halting momentarily to catch his breath, he

listened for pursuit. He expected them to get their horses so they could cover more ground. But they might try to follow him on foot, especially if Bumbry was sure he had wounded him.

Hearing nothing, Lane moved on.

His legs were trembling from weariness and he knew he had to stop and wrap his arm. He found a small gully coming into the main valley and he stopped at its mouth to listen. He heard no pursuit. Maybe he could hide in here and they wouldn't find him in the dark. If he had a chance to rest a while, he could move on before the break of day.

Inside the little gully, which wasn't much wider than six feet, he found a spot where he could drop down and rest. But before he rested, he tore the tail off his shirt and awkwardly wrapped it tightly around his arm. The arm was paining fiercely now, but he was satisfied when he didn't feel the blood oozing through the bandage. If he'd stopped the bleeding, he'd be all right.

His thoughts of gaining revenge on Bumbry and Widlow for killing his brother were fading from his mind. The only thing he had time to think about now was how to escape from the valley. Those two outlaws would try to make sure he didn't survive. They wanted him dead, but before he died, they wanted to force him into telling them where Stella's gold was.

He wanted to stay and fight, but all he had to fight with was a knife and a crippled left arm. If he had a gun, it would be different. The only alternative he saw was to try to sneak away and make a run for the fort. That didn't set well with him. Running was not his way. But he saw no other possibility.

Settling down to wait, he thought of Stella and Bessie. They thought he had stayed behind to try to get the gold that Widlow had stolen from Bessie, and that had been part of his plan. But he also wanted to settle the score with Bumbry and Widlow. So far he hadn't accomplished either. He wondered now if he could even get the gold back to Stella that was hidden down here in the valley. If he didn't get that, would Widlow find it? It seemed uncanny how Widlow managed to come out ahead in every confrontation.

Lane wished he dared go get it. But he knew he'd be lucky just to get back to the fort. Maybe they could come out later with some soldiers and find the gold, if Widlow didn't find it first.

Lane felt that he had let the girls down and was letting his brother, Chris, down, too. How could he live with himself if he had to give up?

He tried to get some sleep, but his arm hurt so much he couldn't even rest. He wiped the knife on the grass. It was his only weapon. But how much good could it do?

After half an hour he began to relax. They must

have gone down the valley looking for him, so he had a reprieve.

As the night wore on and Lane couldn't sleep, he became more restless. He should be trying to get out of the valley while he had darkness as an ally. But he knew that darkness could also be an enemy. If he made any sound, the outlaws might hear it. They were surely on the alert even if they had no idea where he was. And it was hard to travel without making any noise when he couldn't see where he was going.

Dawn found him stiff and feeling miserable. Lane was tired and his arm was still paining him whenever he moved it. He was thankful that it was his left arm that had been struck by the bullet, not his right arm. He got to his feet and slowly worked the sore arm up and down and in small circles. The pain eased a little after he got the arm limbered up, but it still throbbed with every move.

With the light getting stronger, Lane moved out of his little gully, thinking he might go over the hill to another valley and try to get to the fort that way. Bumbry and Widlow obviously had come back through another valley from their fruitless holdup of Dodson's wagon in order to get to Lane's camp before he got there. They hadn't passed Lane last night in this valley.

Outside the little gully, he got a surprise that changed his thinking. He spotted drops of blood on the rocks. His eyes followed those drops and he realized he had left that trail last night. On the grass, the drops weren't so noticeable, but wherever they hit a rock, they stood out like beacons. Once his eye got on the trail, he could follow it even on the grass.

Even if Bumbry and Widlow had expected Lane to go down the valley, they'd change their minds in a hurry if they saw that trail this morning. They would also know that Lane was wounded. They'd track him down as they would a wounded deer.

Lane thought of trying to get away, but he realized they'd follow him now and likely find him before he could escape. Maybe the trail was not so clear farther down the valley. If it was, his one chance would be to backtrack and try to escape detection as the two outlaws followed the trail up the valley. By the time they realized he had backtracked, he might be far enough ahead to get away.

He had no trouble following the trail of blood spots, but he kept a close watch ahead. He didn't want to come face to face with Widlow and Bumbry following the same trail the other way.

He remembered that he had followed the edge of the valley which at times jutted out into a bluff. The bed of the stream cut close to the edge of the valley in places and it was at one of those places where Lane saw the trail run under an overhanging bluff. In the darkness last night, he hadn't realized that he had gone under the overhang. There were rocks underneath the overhang, and the trail there was as plain as print on the page of a book.

Lane's eyes shot up that overhang. It was a chalk-like rock and the top of the outcropping was almost flat. He wondered if he could get up there and lie flat and possibly escape detection when the outlaws came up that trail. There was no doubt in his mind that they would see the trail of blood and follow it. The closer he came to the gully where he had been shot last night, the more distinct the trail became.

Lane backtracked until he found a slope he could climb easily without leaving marks. Then he moved out on the flat-topped overhang and lay down. If Bumbry or Widlow came along this trail and saw him up here, he'd make a target like a duck frozen in ice. But if they didn't see him, they'd follow the trail up the valley while Lane was hurrying down the valley.

Lane could see up and down the valley for some distance from his spot on top of the overhang. If he only had a gun, he could pick off anyone approaching him from either direction. On the other hand, if they spotted him up here, he'd be dead before he could get off the ledge.

The sun soon moved around until it was bearing down on Lane. The heat reflecting off the white rock made the ledge feel like the top of a stove. He began to reconsider his situation. His position was risky at best, but surely he had a better chance of escaping detection up here where they'd least expect him than down in the valley where they would be looking for him.

He worked his left arm occasionally to keep it from getting too stiff. He checked the bandage frequently for signs that the wound had opened up and begun bleeding again. It appeared all right. He was tired and he suspected that was partly weakness from loss of blood plus the lack of sleep last night. But it was certain he couldn't afford to sleep now.

Still, the hot sun was making him drowsy, in spite of the steam bath he felt he was getting. The heat actually felt good on his arm.

Then suddenly he was jerked alert when a movement down in the valley caught his eye. He rolled his head enough to look at the man coming around the curve in the valley wall a hundred yards away.

Lane expected the two outlaws to be together, but Bumbry seemed to be alone as he came up the valley. His eyes were on the ground, skipping from one blood spot to another. Lane realized he had guessed right about that. Sometime this morning they had found the trail of blood spots and now Bumbry was following it. Lane wondered why Widlow wasn't with him.

In a way he was glad that he wasn't. If both men were on the trail, there would be twice the chance that he'd be discovered up here. On the other hand, if Widlow wasn't here, then he was likely down the valley somewhere. If Lane waited until Bumbry was gone, then tried to escape down the valley, he'd likely run into Widlow.

The thoughts chased each other rapidly through Lane's mind. The whole idea of hiding up here was to escape detection until the two men who were after him had gone up the valley, leaving the lower valley open for him to get away. Now it looked as if he'd be caught between the two men if he let Bumbry go up the valley while Widlow stayed somewhere below.

As he watched Bumbry come forward like a bloodhound on a scent, he thought of his brother, Chris, who had died in that ambush. Because of Bumbry.

Lane wished he had a gun. He'd call Bumbry's name before he shot because he'd want him to know why he was being killed.

But Lane was being deprived of that satisfaction. He could hardly challenge Bumbry's gun with his knife. He felt the knife in his belt and a strong urge came over him. He might die trying to carry out his scheme, but he'd inflict some kind of damage on Bumbry in the effort.

Slipping the knife free of his belt, he gripped it fiercely in his right hand. If Bumbry just didn't look up before he passed under the rock! He might go around the overhang, but the trail Lane had left last night went directly under the overhang. Bumbry seemed intent on following the trail of blood spots. Likely he expected to find a helpless man at the end of that trail. Lane didn't doubt that he planned to torture him to find out where the gold was and then kill him.

Lane held his breath, not moving a muscle as Bumbry came closer. All he needed to do was lift his eyes just once and he'd likely see Lane lying on the overhang. But he was concentrating on the trail.

Bumbry stopped ten feet short of the overhang. Lane cringed. If Bumbry was going to check his surroundings, he'd almost certainly look up and see him. The outlaw turned to look back over his course. Then his eyes followed the spots past him and underneath the overhang. He moved closer and when he went out of sight, Lane very quietly rose to his knees, facing the upper valley, the direction Bumbry was going.

But Bumbry didn't come out from under the overhang. Lane waited, the hair on the back of his neck prickling like tiny needles. Where was he? Had he gotten a glimpse of Lane and was now backing out where he could get a shot at him?

Lane slowly turned his head to look back. He couldn't see Bumbry there, either. Bumbry was still under the overhang, but Lane couldn't think why. Surely he must have seen Lane up on the rock and was trying to decide how best to deal with him.

Then he heard a sigh under the rock. Bumbry evidently was relaxing. At least that was what Lane wanted to believe. The sun was warm and that overhang offered good shade. But how long would he stay there before he came out? Lane had to time his move to the precise second if he expected to have any hope of succeeding in his scheme. It was going to be very difficult to perfect that timing when he had no idea when Bumbry would appear.

Lane's legs began to ache as he kept them tensed in a crouch. Still, Bumbry didn't appear. He might even go out the other way, Lane realized. He had to eliminate the negative thoughts and plan on the one move that could succeed. And that would depend on Bumbry as well as Lane.

Lane found he couldn't keep himself so tense any longer and relaxed a bit, but he didn't relax his vigil. Beneath him, he heard a shuffling and rocks sliding. He guessed Bumbry had sat down and was not getting up. Or was he just sitting down?

He heard a big puff that told him Bumbry was exerting some effort. He must be getting to his feet. Once more Lane tensed himself, his eyes glued to the edge of the overhang where Bumbry would first appear if he followed the trail up the valley.

Lane saw the edge of Bumbry's hat first. The relief in knowing he had guessed right almost released the tension in him. But he couldn't afford even the slightest letdown now.

As Bumbry took another step up the valley, he came out from under the overhang. Now was the time.

Lane leaped out over the overhang. Bumbry heard the gravel scrape as Lane launched his leap and he whirled. But Lane was on him by then. They went down in a heap. Lane's right hand held the knife, but he hesitated to use it. He disliked knives intensely. His left hand grabbed for Bumbry's gun, but there was no strength in that arm, only pain.

Bumbry twisted until he could see Lane's face. "You!" he gasped. His hand broke Lane's grip and dug for his gun.

Lane pushed the knife in his face. "Hold it," he snapped.

Bumbry had his gun in his hand now. Lane had no choice. He hated what knives did to people but if anybody deserved to be carved up, it had to be Jud Bumbry.

His knee shot forward and struck Bumbry's gun hand and bent it backward. Then the knife came down. Lane saw the shock in Bumbry's face.

"That's for Chris and all the others you murdered," Lane grunted.

When Bumbry was finally still, Lane was so weak he could hardly crawl away from the big man. His arm ached fiercely. Bumbry had wrenched it when he broke his gun hand free and it was still feeling the results of that.

Lane just wanted to lie down and rest for a day. But he knew he couldn't allow himself even a minute to relax. Bumbry was gone, but he was only half of the duo. Easy Widlow was still somewhere in the valley. He'd come looking for Bumbry soon.

All the vengeance was drained out of Lane now. He'd be happy just to get out of the valley and never see Widlow again. Then he thought of the gold that Widlow had stolen from Bessie. Bessie and Stella needed that to pay off the mortgage on their mine and ranch. It was hard for Lane to realize that it was important now. The most important thing in the world to him was to get someplace where he could safely relax and rest.

But work had to come first. He went back to Bumbry and searched him carefully. He might have the gold. But he discovered that he didn't. That meant that Widlow probably had it. Widlow, the invincible one, according to talk Lane had heard. Widlow was the boss, even of Bumbry. So he surely had kept the gold himself. If Lane was going to help Stella, he had to find Widlow and get that pouch of gold.

He picked up Bumbry's gun as he left and staggered down the canyon. Somewhere down here, he'd run into Widlow. What he expected to do when he met him was vague in his mind. He just knew he couldn't rest until he had met Widlow and made an attempt to get that gold.

It only registered faintly with Lane that the odds were still stacked against him. Easy Widlow was a tough opponent.

Lane reached a beckoning gully. He hesitated for a minute, thinking he might crawl in the gully and rest for just a little while.

The knife slipped from his hand and he stooped to pick it up. At that instant, a bullet split the air where his head had been a second before.

Lane didn't even straighten up. His lethargy vanished and he dived into the gully. He wasn't going to have to look for Widlow. The outlaw had found him. And he had Lane trapped.

XIV

Lane wasn't sure where the bullet had come from. He couldn't see anybody out there. He dived behind a small rock near the opening of the gully. It wasn't very good protection, but, until he could locate where Widlow was, he was afraid to move. He might move out where he was more exposed than he was now.

Then another bullet snapped past Lane. This time he located the source. It had come from the creek bed, which was no more than fifty yards from the mouth of the gully. There wasn't enough water in the creek to keep Widlow from using the bank as a perfect breastworks.

Lane answered Widlow's fire although he doubted if he could hit the target that bobbed up for only a second at a time. Widlow was well below the creek bank when he wasn't shooting.

When Widlow's head popped up for another shot, Lane snapped a bullet at it. He had missed, he knew. He hadn't had time to aim. Still, Lane waited and shot at the outlaw each time he poked his head up.

Neither man was scoring any hits, but Lane didn't give up until the hammer of his gun fell on an empty cylinder. He reached for more shells and realized suddenly that he had picked up

Bumbry's gun, but he hadn't taken his gunbelt. He didn't have any more ammunition.

Down in the creek, Widlow bobbed his head up and took another shot at Lane. But he was farther down the stream now. He was working around to where he would be out of sight of the mouth of the gully where Lane was hiding.

Lane knew he had to move somewhere before Widlow realized he was out of ammunition. Maybe if he got over to the rear of the gully, he could find a way up over the hill and down into another valley that would take him out to the Platte.

He inched around to get out of sight of the last spot where he had seen Widlow. It wouldn't take Widlow long to realize something was wrong because Lane wasn't firing back at him. He wondered if Widlow had guessed something had happened to Jud Bumbry. How else would Lane have gotten a gun?

Lane backed off faster as soon as he thought he was out of sight of Widlow. He didn't know what to expect of the outlaw leader, but he knew he had to use all his wits if he expected to come out alive. If he had more ammunition, he'd be willing to take his chances in a gun duel. But things always seemed to lean Widlow's way. Without a gun, Lane had little chance. Widlow would soon figure that out.

Lane worked his way back into the gully,

searching the slope above him for a way out. It was his own fault. He should have taken Bumbry's ammunition belt when he got his gun. But back then, he was so dazed and the pain in his arm so sharp that he had been fortunate to remember to get the gun. His arm still hurt ferociously, but the peril that was closing in on him had banished any weariness he had felt.

Near the back of the gully, Lane stopped and looked up at the steep slope. Only the little troughs washed there by rain water rushing down into the gully offered any protection at all if he tried to climb out.

Lane didn't know where Widlow was now, but he was willing to bet that he was closing in on the gully. He'd never give up, especially when he realized that Lane was no longer able to shoot at him.

Lane found a small pocket that had been washed out of the side of the gully by a riverlet. It was wide enough for him to squeeze into and be out of sight of anyone near the mouth of the gully.

Lane slipped into it and waited. He could barely see the mouth of the gully. If Widlow came after him, it would have to be through there.

Within three minutes, Widlow showed up, peering cautiously around the corner into the gully, his gun in front of him. If Lane had just had some ammunition, he'd have had a good chance now of beating the outlaw leader to the shot. But maybe Widlow was truly invincible. Luck seemed always to be with him. Right now all Lane could do was wait and hope that Widlow didn't see him.

It was a long time before Widlow ventured into the gully. He had seen Lane near the mouth of the gully, so he had to know that he had backed in here. Widlow had scanned it all carefully with his eyes. Lane saw him flip his eyes up toward the top of the slope behind the gully more than once. If Lane had tried to get out that way, he'd be dead now. He was probably just prolonging the agony this way.

Widlow finally moved into the gully, keeping behind any protection he could find. But as he advanced, he became braver. Obviously he had decided that Lane had either run out of ammunition or the ability to fire the gun.

He probed into every nook he came to, but he kept moving toward Lane. Lane thought of throwing his knife, but he wasn't gifted in that use of the weapon. He'd only give away his position quicker. There was no doubt that Widlow was going to find his hiding place when he got back this far.

Widlow was moving very slowly from one side of the gully to the other, making sure he was not overlooking anything. Each sweep brought him closer to Lane. The next time across the gully, he'd be close enough to see into the pocket where Lane was hiding. Lane had to do something.

Again he thought of throwing the knife, hoping he could hit Widlow with the blade. Then he thought of his empty gun. It didn't have a stabbing edge but it was heavy enough, and he could throw it more accurately. It would make an impression when it hit.

Widlow came to the near wall and then moved back across to the far side to examine every nook over there. When he turned to come back, he'd see Lane. Lane waited until his back was as much to him as it was going to be. Then he stepped out where he had room to throw and, holding the gun by the barrel, he gave it as hard a toss as he could.

Widlow caught the movement and wheeled, bringing his own gun up. He saw Lane apparently a split second before he saw the gun winging through the air. He ducked but too late. The gun hit him on the side of the head.

Lane was running toward Widlow almost before the gun hit its target. He was within twenty feet of Widlow when the metal thing hit him. Widlow's finger on the trigger jerked involuntarily and the bullet shot skyward.

The outlaw didn't go down from the blow, but he reeled backward, totally off balance. Lane hit him before he could recover. He got his good hand on Widlow's gun and wrenched at it. His left hand was almost useless, but it still held the knife. He brought the knife up toward Widlow's gun arm.

Widlow saw the knife and slackened his grip to defend himself against it. Lane wrenched the gun free in that moment. Backing off a step, he dropped the knife and used his weak left hand to turn the gun around so he had the barrel pointed toward Widlow.

"Now what?" Widlow panted, stopping dead in his tracks when he saw his own gun pointed at him.

"That's up to you," Lane said. "You're my prisoner. I'm taking you to the fort."

Widlow was eyeing the gun in Lane's hand, and Lane dropped a sharp glance at it himself. He saw why Widlow was so fascinated by it. Lane's hand was shaking as if he had the ague.

He tried to steady the hand, but he couldn't. The tension of the last few hours and the weakness caused by the loss of blood were getting to him. His left hand was almost useless now. It had been a strain just to grasp the gun while he turned it around for his right hand.

Lane whipped his eyes up to Widlow. The outlaw's eyes were searching Lane's face, obviously estimating his chances of overcoming the advantage Lane had by holding the gun.

In spite of all Lane could do, the gun was sagging in his hand. It seemed as heavy as a barrel of lead. He tried to bring his left hand over to help hold his right hand steady, but it refused to work. And as he concentrated on his left hand, his right hand grew weaker.

Widlow's eyes gleamed and suddenly he lunged toward Lane. Lane had anticipated that move and he concentrated every effort into bringing the gun up. He squeezed the trigger twice as Widlow charged forward.

The first shot jolted Widlow enough to slow him down. Lane had managed to level the gun by the time the second shot was squeezed off. Widlow had lost his gamble. The surprise of it was plain on his face before he rocked back and sank to the ground.

Lane sank down, too, the tension draining from him. His body had reached its limit of endurance, and he rolled over on the ground and the world turned black.

Lane wasn't sure how long he was out, but it didn't seem like any time had passed. The position of the sun told him, however, that at least an hour had elapsed since he had faced Widlow over that gun.

Slowly he sat up. The world spun around at first, but then it settled down and he felt better than he had since he'd been shot. In front of him was Widlow, the Invincible, who had taken his last gamble and lost.

Lane stood up. His arm still hurt but not as

bad as it had before. He was a little unsteady on his feet, but he no longer had to demand such great effort from his muscles and they gradually responded.

He thought of Stella's gold. He had to find that. He searched through Widlow's pockets, but it wasn't there. More than likely the man had it in his saddlebags, but he'd have to find Widlow's horse. He stuck Widlow's gun under his belt.

Leaving the gully, still walking a little unsteadily, he moved down to the creek where Widlow had been when he first shot at Lane. The horse wasn't there, but he was downstream a way in the willows. Apparently Widlow had seen Lane staggering down from his encounter with Bumbry and had hidden his horse and lay in wait for him.

In the saddlebags on the horse, Lane found the pouch of gold. He took the horse and left the gold in the saddlebag. He wondered where his own horse was and where all the horses from the wagons had gone. That would be a chore for the army to find out.

Lane knew his job wasn't finished yet. He had to get the gold that he and Stella had hidden. And it all must be in Omaha in a very short time. He had lost track of the days, so he wasn't sure just when the deadline was. If he could get the gold to Fort McPherson, likely Stella could get it to Omaha on the train. After all the trouble that gold had caused, it would be a shame if it failed by just a few hours to pay off the mortgage.

Lane fought his weakness. He needed to lie down and rest for a full day and night. But he couldn't allow himself that luxury now. He thought of the banker, Atley Robinson, and how arrogant he had been when refusing to take the gold until it was delivered to him in his office in Omaha. Lane hadn't seen the contract, but he didn't doubt that the stipulation was there. A man like Atley Robinson would be sure to have that written in and then hope it would be overlooked when all parties were signing it.

Gripping the saddle horn, he guided the horse down the valley to the spot where he and Stella had hidden the gold. With each step the horse took toward the hiding place, his worry increased that someone might have found the gold.

The hiding place was undisturbed, however, and Lane lifted off the rock. The three bags of gold were there and he put them in the saddlebag with the other pouch.

Now he faced the long trek to Fort McPherson. He should feel good about it. There were no outlaws waiting in ambush for him now. They had run out their string. Lane's biggest enemy now was his own weakness. It had been a hard few days and that wound last night that had bled so freely had drained away most of his ambition and much of his stamina.

Clinging to the saddle horn with his right hand, he guided the horse with pressure of his knees and started him at a good walk down the valley and then turned east down the Platte valley toward the fort.

He was sure he would have passed out a time or two except for the pain in his left arm which kept him aware of his surroundings.

Lane didn't remember that it was so far from the valley to the fort. He hung on, fighting a nausea that threatened to dump him out of the saddle. Then, just as he recognized his surroundings and knew he was within a few miles of the fort, he met a column of soldiers. Sergeant Dodson was in the lead.

Lane explained briefly what had happened back in the valley. "What happened to Private Lyon and the reinforcements he was to bring us?"

"His horse stepped in a hole and threw him then ran off," Dodson said. "Lyon got lost and just limped in to the post this morning. Do you have all the gold?"

Lane nodded. "It has to be in Omaha soon."

"Tomorrow is the deadline," Dodson said. "Atley Robinson keeps reminding everybody. He's at the fort."

Lane perked up. "Then we can settle this quickly for the girls."

Dodson turned the column around and they headed back to the fort. Lane looked for the girls as soon as they reached the parade. The fort was not an enclosed fort but merely had the necessary buildings surrounded by flat river bottomland and hills to the south. Neither of the girls was in sight. But Atley Robinson was present. Lane remembered him vividly.

Dodson dismissed the soldiers and rode with Lane to meet Robinson who was coming to see why the soldiers were returning.

"I've got the gold for you," Lane said to the banker. "You can burn that mortgage now."

Robinson scowled. "Not so fast. That money has to be delivered to me in my office in Omaha by tomorrow."

"Then you'd better be in your office tomorrow," Lane said.

"There's no way you're going to get that money to Omaha by tomorrow," Robinson said smugly.

"Does that contract say that you forfeit the money if it is in your office on time and you're not there?" Dodson asked angrily.

Robinson drew himself up rigidly. "It does not. If the money is there, I'll be there."

"Then you'd better be on the next train to Omaha because this gold will be."

Robinson grinned. "I happen to know there won't be another passenger train through until tomorrow. It won't make it to Omaha before banking hours close. So I'll just stay here and foreclose on that mortgage here."

"Watch that varmint," Dodson said to Lane. "If he gives you any excuse, shoot him." He rode off toward the post headquarters.

Robinson looked after him indignantly. Lane paid little attention to the banker. He was searching for the girls. They should hear the good news that he had arrived with their gold. But Dodson arrived back on the scene before the girls showed up. He had a captain with him.

"The colonel told me to tell you that if you won't accept the money here, you can't issue any foreclosure notices here, either," the captain said.

"I'll have you know I can conduct my business anywhere I please," Robinson said haughtily.

"Good," the captain said. "In that case, you can accept your payment and cancel that mortgage right here on the fort grounds."

The banker gasped. "I'll do as I please about that."

"Think it over, Mr. Robinson," the captain said. "Frankly, the colonel is about fed up with you. He doesn't care whether you leave here on your own two feet or in a pine box."

Robinson looked at the captain, then at Sergeant Dodson and Lane. Both had their hands on their guns. Slowly he wilted.

"You can make the transaction in the colonel's office," the captain said. He led the way across the grounds with the banker shuffling along behind him.

"I'll get the girls," Dodson said. "They should be the ones to take the gold in and close the deal."

Lane waited as Dodson went to one of the barracks. In a minute both Stella and Bessie came out into the sunshine. It was Lane's turn to gasp.

If Stella hadn't been with Bessie, he wasn't sure that he would have recognized her. Her hair was rolled up at the front of her head and the long ends done up in a bun on the back of her head. She had on a blue dress that Lane guessed was ordinarily reserved for parties. What he had thought were rather plain features were suddenly beautiful. Clothes didn't make the girl but they did help to make her looks.

Lane strode toward her, almost forgetting the pain in his arm. He stopped a few feet from her. "Your hair," he stuttered. "Your dress—your—your eyes—you're beautiful."

"Glad you finally noticed," Bessie said.

Lane barely heard her. "Your—your—Oh, I've got your gold here. Sergeant Dodson has made arrangements for you to meet Robinson in the colonel's office and pay him off and cancel the mortgage."

"Wonderful," Stella said. Then her eyes fell on his arm. "You're hurt."

"Never mind that," Lane said. "Just let me look at you. Why did you dress up like this? What's going on?"

"Bessie fixed me up," Stella said.

"How can you be so blind?" Bessie said. "Stella didn't want to welcome you back dressed like a tramp."

Suddenly it hit Lane. Stella was fixed up just to greet him. If he hadn't known it before, he knew it now. Stella was the one woman for him.

"Let's fix that arm," Stella said, concern in her voice.

"First things first," Lane said. "First, get rid of that mortgage. Then you and I have some things to talk about. Then we'll tend to the arm."

"I can't imagine what we have to talk about," she said mischievously.

"Try hard to imagine it," Lane said. "It will save us a lot of time."

About the Author

Wayne C. Lee was born in Lamar, Nebraska. Until 1951, he was a farmer, and he noted, "writing had to be just a spare-time hobby." Upon becoming a rural mail carrier out of the Lamar post office, he devoted more time to writing. Though he did not receive a degree, he took correspondence courses from the University of Nebraska and a writing course in a summer session at Western State College, in Colorado.

For many years, Lee was on the board of the Nebraska State Historical Society and Chase County Historical Society, and he was once vice president of Western Writers of America. The author wrote dozens of books, hundreds of short stories, plays and poems, and 400-plus songs. A prolific writer of Western fiction, Wayne's *Wild Towns of Nebraska* and his *Bad Men and Bad Towns* are among his best-known nonfiction titles.

Center Point Large Print
600 Brooks Road / PO Box 1
Thorndike, ME 04986-0001 USA

(207) 568-3717

US & Canada:
1 800 929-9108
www.centerpointlargeprint.com